TRIXIE TRASH,

STAR ASCENDING

TRIXIE TRASH,

STAR ASCENDING

Tom Wakefield

Routledge & Kegan Paul
London and Henley

First published in 1977
by Routledge & Kegan Paul Ltd
39 Store Street,
London WC1E 7DD and
Broadway House,
Newtown Road,
Henley-on-Thames,
Oxon RG9 1EN
Set in 11 on 13 Baskerville 169 by
Kelly and Wright, Bradford-on-Avon, Wiltshire
and printed in Great Britain by
Lowe & Brydone Ltd
© Tom Wakefield 1977

British Library Cataloguing in Publication Data

Wakefield, Tom
Trixie Trash, star ascending.
I. Title
823' .9' 1F   PR6073.A/
ISBN 0-7100-8574-5

For
My Niece
Paula and
Margaret

Star of wonder, star of night
Star of Royal beauty bright
Westward leading still proceeding
Guide us to . . .

INTRODUCTION

'Shovel one. Shovel two. Shovel one, two, three, shovel one, shovel two and stamp and stamp and clap. Cha-ss-ay to the left, shovel one and stamp and clap. Lovely, try it once more, girls. Hold yourselves up straight. Hold yourselves up straight. Keep in time with the piano and watch your breathing as you sing or you'll lose your smiles.'

Gloria Jones, principal, and sole teacher of the Glorianna Dancing School, hypnotised the thirty-five girl soldiers before her as they went through their final rehearsal. Her demonstration was precise and without fault, her forty-seven-year-old frame shook rather than wobbled as there was not an ounce of spare flesh on it. No one had any clear idea of what she really looked like, a mask had been painted over her face all the time that she had been performing in Runnock, and that was at least seventeen years. Locally, she was very popular. She had never been seen not smiling.

Her school of dance which had begun modestly in a broken down pavilion on the park had prospered. She now leased a hall and a rehearsal room from the local Co-operative Society. The clanging cash registers from the shops beneath did not in any way deter her from creative onslaught. Classes were held every week-night and all day Saturday, a tiring but very lucrative schedule that left her little spare time.

There was the 'Happiness Club' for the tiny tots (three to seven years) between five and six. This was followed by the 'Future Stars Group' (seven to twelve years) between half past six and a quarter to eight. She rested during week days and most evenings after work studied her accounts. However, during the late evenings of Wednesdays and Thursdays, she sometimes visited her piano accompanist Arthur. Occasionally, she stayed the whole evening with him. She felt obliged to do this as his wages had not risen according to her profits. His physical demands took less out of her than a tap session and his love-making did not manage to indent her smile; quite often, she was hardly aware of it going on. There was no doubt about it, Arthur was a bargain; as for Gloria Jones, she was first and foremost an artiste, and in this respect, there was no question of her lacking two fundamental requirements – dedication and discipline.

'Well, girls, we are all ready for the show, there's no need for any of you to be nervous. You know the routines.' She wagged a cautionary finger.

'Remember, when we go into the hall, you are all on stage. No talking through the performance, no whispering, and if any of you want to go to the lavatory, go now, because it's not allowed once the show has begun. Everybody ready, let me see your smiles, chins up.'

She led her troupe confidently into the hall and assembled them behind the curtain on the rickety platform stage. Their behaviour was perfect, she felt quite confident. Nothing ever did go wrong as her training had slashed away any kind of free expression or natural grace. The girls shuffled themselves into groups, and the puppeteer nodded to Arthur to indicate that she was ready to pull the strings.

'Oh, that's a bit better.' Florrie Davis settled herself with a great deal of effort on to the plastic chair in the front row of the stalls. The back and seat sagged under her weight, but held. Parts of Florrie billowed over onto the seats either side of her and the occupants of both seats were forced to edge over a bit in order to let the elderly barrage balloon settle. Florrie caught her breath and placed her paper carrier bag at her feet. These were swollen with illness and casually encased in a pair of old brown checked slippers. Sensitive to the discomfiture of her neighbours, Florrie offered placation.

'Like a peppermint, duck?' She ignored the frozen smiles and shaking heads of the two women and continued to talk as she popped a sweet into her own mouth.

'I thought I'd never get 'ere in time, all the buses kept going past full. Awful 'ent it, when you want to get somewhere important? I got myself in a right state, all aerated, you can see, with legs like mine, my walking days are over. Mr Simpson the Co-op grocer-man gave me a lift. So 'ere I am, on time, but what a game.'

She sucked her mint, mindful that little notice was being taken of her. She was not deterred.

'It's worth it, though, I wouldn't have missed my Margaret for the world. She looked a picture this morning. Gave me a little show all to myself, oh, she is clever. She's a treasure, all I've got but. . . .' One of the women interrupted Florrie who had lapsed into soliloquy.

'She's not yer own is she, luv?'

The question acquired more cruelty with the sweetness of its delivery. Both women turned to Florrie hoping to see some measure of pain flicker across the plump contented face. If there had been injury it did not show.

'She's more mine than my own daughter was. I'm happier now than when my husband was alive. All thanks to my Margaret – a treasure she is.'

'I think I've met her, a bit "old-headed" isn't she?' said her neighbour as she put a trace of powder on her nose. Florrie sat and smiled. The piano began to bang out an overture.

'She's as she wants to be, duck, and that's more than good enough for me. Are you sure you won't 'ave a peppermint?'

Both women took one. Slain by kindness, they sulked until the curtain rose.

A cyclorama of plastic flowers intertwined on thin wooden lattice (originally intended for roses) served as a permanent back cloth for the stage. Most of the flowers had come from 'free offers' with soap powders – Gloria had asked the students to bring them along. Response was magnificent and the enduring blooms had begun to creep along the edge of the stage. An unfinished trail also threatened to engulf Arthur with honeysuckle. The stage itself was void of furnishings, save for an enormous drum, three feet high and five feet in diameter. This was placed centrally. Its effect drew an appreciative gasp from the audience as Arthur hammered out a suitably military introduction on the piano.

There's something about a soljer
There's something about a soljer
There's something about a soljer, that is fine, fine, fine.

The girls were right on cue and though their voices lacked sweetness, there was no doubt about its message or delivery, as the tap-dancers swung into line. Short blue satin dresses revealed dimpled fleshy thighs which shook as they tapped. A pink sash coupled with a pink busby and red tap-shoes served to provide the regiment's ammunition. The sparks flew from their feet as they sang, stamped and clapped. The solo or central performer was distinguished by a reversal of colour scheme. Her dress was pink, the rest of her was blue, and she remained in the centre of the line. A discerning eye might have noticed that she was no more efficient than the rest of the girls. Indeed, she appeared to have a slight weight problem which placed her well below average. However, Gloria considered her quite a find as Sandra's father was the only local estate agent, and her mother was on the Council. It might be possible to raise fees again if more pupils of Sandra's class would enrol, it might give the school added tone.

There's something about 'is wearing
There's something about 'is bearing, that is fine, fine, FINE.

It was only after the last line had been repeated five times and after 'fine' had been shrieked so loud by the chorus that the shops beneath had heard it, that the audience felt that something was going slightly wrong. In fact, the poor dancing girls were awaiting a finale sequence which persisted in never arriving. Each time they duly circled the drum and gave Sandra her cue word as well as pointing to the drum. Each time Sandra's feet remained firmly fixed to the stage. The magic of the moment had filled her with trepidation so that the height of the drum had suddenly taken on enormous proportions for her. She remained with face smiling and feet frozenly tapping the stage.

Florrie knew it was against the rules, but she couldn't resist waving to the perky, thin little girl four to the left of Sandra. Her Margaret took this as a sign for a relaxation on the code of discipline and conduct, and without a trace of hesitation leapt on to the drum. The chorus line faltered and Sandra's feet stopped tapping all together – this had never happened in rehearsal and Gloria Jones never trained understudies. She stood in the wings sickened and bewildered by the change in routine. It was Arthur, who had spoken rarely to any of the girls, who hissed from the piano, 'Salute, salute.' A grin flickered across his face as the corps obeyed and gave their new trumpet major her proper due. Flushed with pride and esteem, Margaret delivered the solo on the drum as of right; not until

5

the Union Jack finally unfurled itself at the back of the stage did her feet stop. The rapturous applause rang through the hall and tremors of joy ebbed and flowed through Florrie Davis whose legs and feet had meticulously shed their weight and pain throughout the performance.

'Can I keep my uniform on, Auntie?'

'Course, course you can, darlin'. Put your coat on when we go out, we don't want yer to ketch cold. You can tek it off when we get on the bus so as folks can see yer. Then when we get to Hancock Street, we'll call on Mrs Shirley. She'd love to see yer, I'll get two milk stouts and you can have pop and crisps. Oh, it was lovely. You were grand, duck, grand.'

Florrie lumbered from the hall with Margaret trailing on her arm. The two were always seen this way, both were oblivious to criticism from any quarter; neighbourhood and school could never divide or dislocate their proximity. Consequently, Florrie's death six years later left Margaret marooned. In this sense, it was as well that she had learned to tap-dance as this formal training, coupled with an innate ability to improvise, served to stand her in good stead for the future.

PART ONE

PART ONE

'I thought it all went off very nicely.'

Cora was referring to her mother's funeral.

'Almost all the curtains in the street were drawn. That Mrs Shirley came out in her slippers and kept waving to the cars, did you see her? I pretended not to. Oh, some people are common, they've no sense of occasion. She was supposed to be a friend of me mother's – I don't know. Still "Louise's", the hairdresser on the corner, added a nice touch, did you notice? There was black crepe round the window and over the wigs. The least said about our Margaret the better, all that crying and fainting in church, you'd have thought she was my mother's real daughter, not me – and then not coming to the reception afterwards. She was in Mrs Shirley's playing pontoon. What a way to pay your last respects.'

'Terrible', said Len who always agreed with his wife.

'I don't know why she took the girl on in the first place.

You know how stubborn me mother could be, she would never tell whose she was – no never. What she's said to the girl about it is as closed as a book. We'll get no truck out of her though if we asked all year. She's a funny one, all that dancing and the way she acts up. She's been a May Queen, a Milk Queen, a Coal Queen, the Labour Queen. It's just embarrassing, she's clever though, she learned to type in a year – that last year at school. She's a good job at Barraclough & Perris the solicitors, if only she'll stick at it. She can afford good board, Len, she won't need a lot for spending at her age. The money she brings in will pay for the central heating.'

Their human premium bond sat on the front lawn of 27 Tree Tops Avenue; from where she sat there were no trees visible. Opposite her was a bungalow with an identical lawn, bordered by identical clumps of gladioli. Margaret glared at the grinning gnomes whose plaster faces seemed to enjoy her present state of discontent. On her arrival, she had liked the name painted on the gate. 'Corlen' – she had imagined that it represented a lovely sea-bird and the idea that a house had a name rather than a number appealed to her imagination. The sea-bird had become distinctly tar-stained, and in fact, had sunk to the bottom of the ocean, when she discovered that the bird represented Cora and Len from its tail feathers to its beak.

Margaret rubbed her arms as the chill of the late afternoon dappled her with goose pimples, the cold finally won and she rose to enter the house. A gnome positioned three yards to the left of her grinned maliciously and Margaret decided he should not get away with it completely. She grabbed the hideous plaster-cast by its pointed ears and attempted to turn it round, it refused to budge. There was a cracking sound and Margaret spun to the ground holding only his left ear.

'Need any help?'

Startled, Margaret picked herself up and was relieved to

see Arthur the pianist leaning on the front gate. She recovered herself quickly, the black arm band he was wearing caught her attention.

'It's for Gloria,' he added quickly as he caught her gaze. 'Died, just a day after your Auntie.'

'I'm sorry, I didn't know.'

'Nobody seemed to know, there was only me and her cousin at the funeral.'

'She always seemed so healthy, a lovely figure. . . .'

Arthur butted in.

'Ah, that's where people were fooled, it was only her courage kept her going. It wasn't a case of her having a good figure, it was more a question of her having no body. She's been wastin' away for years. Leukaemia you know, but she wouldn't give in to it. She danced her "Four Leaf Clover" routine for the old folks only three days before she passed away.'

His voice trembled and he blew his nose hard into his handkerchief.

'I expect you miss her', Margaret faltered. 'I mean, you must have meant a lot to each other.'

She lied compassionately, as she had always felt that Gloria had treated Arthur like a postage stamp. Give him a lick now and then and he was useful. Her indifference to him had shocked Margaret. Before one performance Gloria had blown dust off the top of the piano right into Arthur's face. He had suppressed his discomfort by turning purple, but not a splutter or cough emerged. As the chorus line giggled, Margaret had wondered whether such loyalty was good for Gloria, but Gloria never seemed to notice such things. For her, Arthur was part of the mechanism that made up the piano.

'Yes, I've always been drawn to theatricals, I know talent when I see it.'

His pale brown, almost yellow eyes beamed from the grey complexion.

'They never let you down, you know. I thought my playing days were over with Gloria, gone, but I'm playing Friday,

Saturday and Sunday at the Utics Nest. When you're a bit older call in and see me, it's a busy pub.'

He turned to leave and the sun caught his shiny pin-stripes. Margaret called after him.

'Is it well paid, Arthur?'

'Yes, yes, it is, and I've Mrs Menton to thank for that.'

He stared at Margaret more deeply and she clutched an imaginary cardigan around her shoulders and small breasts in mild embarrassment.

'You should visit Mrs Menton. She teachers drama and speech at the Mining College. You know, love, you've got the quality. I can always recognise the quality. Lena'd bring it out. The classes are held every Saturday morning.'

Arthur turned and walked away quickly, humming a tune that could have been fifty songs rolled into one. Content that he had been useful, he smiled and treated himself to a cigarette.

After a frugal supper, Margaret left Cora and Len to enjoy their television. They were ecstatically watching a couple from Scunthorpe win hundreds of pounds getting ping-pong balls into goldfish bowls. They were unaware of her departure. Margaret entered her bedroom, sat down and looked at herself. There wasn't really much alternative as the dressing table mirror faced the bed, the expanse between the two being about two or three feet. She tuned into her radio.

'When you're in love, the little things are great. When you're in love, the little things can't wait. The little things, the little things. . . .'

Margaret considered the song which sobbed from the radio and looked about her.

The few photographs didn't seem any bigger, her frocks looked just the same hanging behind the door, and the suitcase on top of the wardrobe looked as though it would stay up there forever. There was no Aunt Florrie to prattle to, she didn't think she could cry any more. Or laugh for that matter and, according to the wireless, the only way to change things was to fall in love. How on earth did you do that? Dancing; everybody that she had known had done it at the Co-op Dance.

'You meet them at the Co-op in March and marry 'em in December, if you're lucky. The thing is not to get yourself caught in between.'

That's what Mrs Shirley had said about it, but Margaret had been to the Co-op Hall the last two Saturdays and, apart from a few bruises, still felt roughly the same as she did before.

She always enjoyed getting ready for the dance more than the dance itself – so much so that on her first visit, she only managed to get herself to it just twenty minutes before the end. Len couldn't understand how she had taken four and a half hours to appear in a white blouse and black skirt, but it wasn't until she had been through all her wardrobe that Margaret had finally decided to wear her old school uniform for the dance. After this, Margaret considered her wardrobe on a Wednesday which meant she could arrive in splendour by eight in the evening on the following Saturday. It was like having two nights for the price of one. Like most people in Runnock, Margaret was forced by circumstance to be thrifty.

She caressed her clothing; this made her feel a little sad because at least half of it would no longer fit her and the very things that she was most fond of, she had worn when she was about ten. The thought of the wasted frills and bows, the tiny print flowers and red tap shoes gave her considerable distress. How cruel it all was, as a little girl she could always dress up as a young lady, but now that she was a young lady, there was no dressing down. Auntie Florrie had always said that she could be whoever she wanted to be and she had often been somebody else for a time. Every year until she was fourteen, she had won £3 in the Labour Party Rally Fancy Dress Parade. She had always looked forward to it, she loved prizes and over the years, she had come to regard the £3 as part of her annual budgeting. It had come as a great shock to her that reaching a certain age denied her access of entry to the competition. It was necessary for her to lie (by a margin of two days), for her to effect her final entrance and exit. A great deal of time and personal sacrifice went into her last triumphant march as Queen Elizabeth I. None of her clothes had ever been discarded or given away and with quiet determination and some pleasure, Margaret unhooked the basis of Queen Elizabeth's costume from the bulge of clothes that were hanging behind the bedroom door which had been transferred into a wardrobe overflow. It had originally started its life as a bridesmaid's gown for Mrs Shirley's daughter, and now it lay in faded peacock-blue splendour crippled by time. One of the hip panniers that she and Aunt Florrie had hoisted into the sides had detached itself and hung limply without purpose, the patterns of sequinned roses had shed so many individual sparkles that they had lost all form and didn't resemble any-thing at all. The huge collar retained only half of its gossamer dignity, the other half had curled back as if to hide itself in shame. It had taken three whole months to make. Margaret had given Aunt Florrie history lessons through all this industry and Aunt Florrie had sat and smiled and listened. The dress lay like a great broken butterfly. Margaret took it up in her arms and more sequins showered to the floor. . . .

'How could you do this to us, Margaret? I had thought that you were such a nice girl. Whatever do you think people are going to say about the type of girl that comes to this school if you come in looking like that? Whatever was your mother – er, I'm sorry, your Aunt, whatever was she doing to let you do such a thing to yourself?'

Miss Simling, headmistress of Lime Pit Lane Secondary Modern Girls' School, looked down at the unmarked blotting paper on her desk disguising her anger and revulsion with the sight before her with an expression of pained anguish and personal grief. She looked for some sign of penitence from the long-necked fourteen-year-old girl perched on the edge of her seat looking for all the world like an impudent flamingo. Miss Simling attacked again, her annoyance and irritability taking away any subtleties she may formerly have possessed.

'It is not as though you have broken one school rule – but two. How you could dye your hair and make that mess of it as well as having your ears pierced with those horrid rings I don't know. I have it in mind to visit the shop that was responsible for it.'

'My Auntie did them with a cork and a needle and she permed my hair like this. I dyed it myself.'

Margaret shook her head as she spoke, but maintained some regal dignity in face of the onslaught.

Miss Simling lowered her standards further.

'Well, you look like a common little tart, I hate to say it, but you look like, just that . . . a common little tart.'

If she hated saying it, then why say it twice, thought Margaret. It was not for her to reply to such ill abuse and, in answer, she raised her head higher and patted her tight orange-red curls with her left hand. Miss Simling's neck changed colour as Margaret's new found autocracy declared itself.

'Unless your hair is covered and the ear-rings are gone by tomorrow, then I must suspend you. You know what this will mean? You do know how serious the consequences will be for you?'

By this time, victory had come to England and the Spanish threats meant nothing to Young Bess. Margaret had already stood without bidding.

'You can do what you like, Miss Simling. I may have the looks of a nice little girl, but I have the heart of a woman. Whatever you decide to do, you must know that I forgive you' – and with one sad glance at her assailant, Margaret left the study for Aunt Florrie and Hancock Street.

Miss Simling picked up the telephone.

'Hello, Miss Simling here, could you give me the school psychological section please. . . .'

As she waited for a reply, she viewed her clear varnished nails, they might look better a shade darker or perhaps even cherry red. She smiled and put down the 'phone. In her own interests it might be as well to forgive Margaret; the girl might be famous one day, distinct histrionic ability. Certainly; and she, Angela Simling, had been the first to recognise it.

From the moment Margaret climbed on to Jack Westwood's decorated coal lorry, she knew that she would triumph. 'Oh, our Margaret', was all Auntie Florrie could say and Mrs Shirley substituted talk for tears. Cheers and laughter greeted the other floats, but when Queen Elizabeth passed by, the crowds were reduced to an awed silence, even her attendants realised the importance of this, her last rally. Dignity was maintained even to the prize-giving ceremony on the bandstand at the park when she collected her £3 as though she were bestowing yet another knighthood. It was hours later when Aunt Florrie laid the dress on the bed.

'Well, Margaret, you've done well, better than ever, your last one better than ever.'

'My last. . . .'

'Oh, you'll be too old next year, love, it's sad when all the dressing up is over, 'ent it? . . .'

Margaret reflected on Aunt Florrie's words as she bent and picked up the sequins one by one. The exercise soothed her and she managed to put away the shattered dress calmly and continued diligently to undress and prepare for bed. It didn't really matter what you wore for the dance, nothing mattered too much now. Aunt Florrie was gone. No, not gone but dead, poor thing and Cora and Len not even wearing a mourning arm-band. Margaret put out the light, but before she closed her eyes she smiled; she had decided that she would wear black for the dance; black jumper, black stockings and a black skirt.

'No, Len, me back hurts something terrible, I knocked myself
on the counter at work on Saturday – we're so busy on Satur‑
day. You can't rely on the part-timers.'

So saying, Cora moved Len's hand from her bottom and put
her own two pink-fringed pillows firmly into position for
sleeping. Len accepted her rejection domestically just in the
same way as he always did the washing up. After all they both
worked. It had been long since agreed that the best night for
Len to do that sort of thing to her was a Wednesday. In this
way, it wouldn't spoil the week-end, and mid-week she was
not too tired. This was the third Wednesday Cora had done
without it, she'd had a woman's private time last week, and
the week before she'd had a sick headache. Whatever that silly
doctor had said at the Runnock Ladies' Fore-Runners Club
about husbands and wives needing it, Cora dismissed as she
tightened her curl net. She must mention to Mrs Lindon that

the 'girls' didn't like it nearly as much as the talk on flower arrangements. For her own part, Cora didn't like any talks much, because she hated listening. She lowered herself carefully on the pillows. She always slept flat on her back, her hair held much better if she did. Sleeping this way was economical, as it meant that she only needed to have her hair burnt once every three weeks and she knew Len admired her for it. She had always been thrifty.

'There's some nice lean bacon for breakfast tomorrow', said Cora smoothing down the counterpane.

'Good', Len felt once again how lucky he was to be with Cora. He would never have left Hancock Street if it hadn't been for her. She was a cut above the rest and had proved it. They would soon have a car for the garage at the present rate of saving. The car and the thought of bacon demolished all thoughts of passion. That kind of thing only came over him once in a while; sometimes, after it had happened, he wished it had never come over him at all. He didn't like to lose his sense of what was right and the last time Cora had been sick afterwards. It had made him feel terrible; she was such a good girl. Feeling much happier, he set the alarm (which also boiled up two cups of tea when it rang) for seven and prepared to settle for conjugal sleep. It was usual procedure for him to let Cora drop off first because of his snoring and, like the good husband he was, he waited.

Breakfast at 'Corlen' always seemed noisy. Cora spent every morning mapping out the day's budget and wondering what the evening meal would be. Margaret never answered the open questions as she knew what the meal would be by the day of the week. It was Friday, so it was fish and chips and that was that. Len made more noise than Cora just by eating and Margaret witnessed the daily morning pattern of bacon rinds circling his plate. She and Cora only had bacon on a Sunday, so on week days she had time to consider Len's dentures as they clicked and negotiated the loving meal that Cora had prepared.

18

Departure from the house was effected at alarm-call pace. Len left seven minutes before Cora.

'Well, I'd best be off, don't want to be late.'

Cora always repeated this afterwards.

'Well we'd best be off, Margaret, we don't want to be late.'

It was impossible for Margaret to be late – in fact leaving with Cora meant that she arrived at her office forty minutes before anyone else. Cora had often been informed of this fact, but either chose to ignore the appeal for morning clemency, or delivered a lecture on wasted electricity.

Margaret parted company with Cora by travelling upstairs on the bus. Here she enjoyed herself for ten minutes by drawing on the steamed-up windows and sometimes writing an extremely rude word and rubbing it out before anyone could see.

Barraclough & Perris were long-established solicitors and their names were known to most of Runnock. As they were the only solicitors in Runnock, this was not surprising. They spoke the language of the law and as most people in Runnock, like most people in Britain, did not understand this language, they revered the families of Barraclough & Perris greatly. Customers or clients attending the office spoke in whispers, they never questioned counsel or advice, mainly because they couldn't understand what was being said. Barraclough & Perris were considered to be very wise. The older Mr Perris was an Independent on the Council. Margaret thought that all of them were stupid. The younger Mr Barraclough sometimes pinched her bottom as though he were doing her a favour. On such days he would recompense his actions by giving her 3p for a jam doughnut to have with her tea.

Making tea and shopping took up a great deal of her office activity. Her working quarters were as restricted as her domestic ones. She was trapped in a triangle of long heavy desks. On two of the desks sat the younger Barraclough and the younger Perris. The younger Perris had never spoken to her directly and probably never would. The younger Barraclough, who was twenty-two years of age, dressed as though he were forty-five years old, and always pitched his voice as low as he possibly could. He addressed her as Miss Davis, but had not yet managed to pitch his voice low enough to get the 's' out, so that to him, she came out as Miss Davy. Margaret was sure that eventually he would swallow his own neck. The last desk was occupied by Miss Wilmot (seventeen years with the firm). Only Miss Wilmot was allowed to take papers into the inner sanctum where the older members of the firm sat. Occasionally Miss Wilmot would come out of the sanctum and sigh,

'Oh, yes he's a wonderful man', or 'I don't know how he does it.'

Which of the two she spoke of, Margaret did not enquire. She didn't have time to, because this was the only verbal indulgence that Miss Wilmot allowed herself before she approached her typewriter and let fling at it as though she were playing a Scarlatti sonata.

The door behind Margaret led to the kitchen. A nod from Miss Wilmot would indicate that tea was needed and fingers were held up as to the required number. Conversation in the office was restricted to variabilities of the weather; the only other noises to be heard were rustling of paper, clacking typewriters, and the roar of the traffic outside. The small window to her left provided some relief for she could look out on to Runnock, or at least she could look at the 1914–1918 War Memorial which towered over the subterranean public lavatories. Four stone defenders struggled to hold up a flag and a stone woman rolled bandages at their feet. This group was perched on a black lead stand which named all the officers and men of Runnock who had died in the war. Six hundred and twelve people had died – Margaret had counted them all. Nine of these were officers, the rest were men. Margaret assumed that the nine officers must have died differently. The Memorial never bored her, but the people going to the lavatory underneath it never gave it a glance before or afterwards. She had checked this. She was fond of the statue as it represented the only fragment of emotion that ever passed through her working day. At first she had imagined that her time might be taken up with typing out details of crimes against person and state, but no such papers had ever come her way. Endless contracts on house purchase were her fate and, after the first three letters, the facts blurred and all houses became one house, and each house constituted a prison for her. Eager to escape, she pounded the typewriter with vigour in order to be free and stare. The staring interludes became more rare, because Miss Wilmot became ill at ease if Margaret were still. If the bank of industry ran dry then Margaret was ordered to make tea. Sometimes, as a last resort, it was requested of her to dust the office.

'Is my D.A. right, Marg?'

Of the thirty or so girls preparing to enter the arena of the Runnock Co-op dance at least half were wearing black. This gave Margaret a moment's pause for thought – they couldn't all be in silent mourning, could they? There was not much time for reflection as she carefully examined the head of the girl next to her and the girl behind Margaret did likewise. Within twenty minutes, the powder room of the tit-and-bum bar (as it was sometimes rudely referred to) was emptied out on to the dance hall for another set of maidens to prepare for the fray. Why the back of every girl's head had to resemble a duck's arse was a source of mystery to most of the girls them-selves, but it was the fashion, so they complied, and 200 reverse duck-heads swam out on to the sea of fortune with drop ear-rings the size of anchors to serve as ballast through any pending storms.

The enormous whirling mirrored ball which spun from the middle of the hall lit up bits of ear, breast, ankle and leg through the smoke and semi-darkness. For the first half hour or so it was difficult to distinguish anyone unless they had some defined physical deformity. It was a mixed dance, but for most of the time the dancers were segregated, the girls often dancing together for the quick-step or the tango and sometimes dancing in groups of three or four for free jive sessions. The males stood in groups like newly arrived immigrants desperate to merge, but afraid to shed their chrysalis before taking flight. Nylon blouses, nylon shirts, nylon underwear, mingled with California Poppy and Lily of the Valley helped to make the air somewhat nauseous, but also exciting. About twelve couples clung to each other fiercely throughout all these preliminaries. These were declared 'engaged' couples and their mutual ownership was flaunted as proof of their superiority and indifference to all the other inmates in the hall, not even an excuse-me quick-step could separate these couples. It was accepted, perhaps with ill-will in some quarters, that they had moved on. By half past nine, Margaret felt tired. She had not missed a dance, but only one had been taken up with a member of the opposite sex and in this case it didn't really count as Freddie Haycock was supposed to be her cousin. Audrey Fenley had held her closer than Freddie and Audrey was a girl.

'All the townies are coming in now, they've been drinking in the Swan. They won't let them in after ten o'clock because they spoil everything. Pauline was in a terrible state because she let. . . .'

Audrey, in spite of her trepidation, was busy adjusting her bra a bit tighter as she spoke to Margaret who viewed the fresh influx of men with curiosity rather than alarm.

'Dance?', before Margaret could answer or look up. She was pulled forward and assembled like components on a conveyor belt. Her neck was cupped in a large hand and her bottom was encased in another. All that she could see in front of her was a multi-coloured tie and a shirt that had two buttons open. Hairs sprouted from the shirt space like cacti and tiny beads of sweat appeared to give them bloom. A glance to the left to seek assurance from Audrey only confirmed that fate had dealt her the same blow. The lights spun, the waltzes droned on and Margaret relaxed into the great hands that encircled her like a seedling finding earth.

'D'you like the band?' The body spoke midway through the third waltz and cued itself to get even closer to Margaret.

'Mm-mm', was all she could say. Her nose was touching the hairs now, her left foot had been crunched twice on the turn, something was sticking in her side and she had great difficulty in breathing.

'I suppose you've been warned about me. It's most likely true what they say, so don't say I haven't told yer.'

The dance had ended and for the first time Margaret was able to see her partner. He towered above her. The suit was brown and smart, but his shirt was undone and the knot in his tie hung on a level with his shoulders, one of his cuff-links was missing and locks of greasy black hair fell on to his forehead. The eyes were large, grey and somewhat bloodshot – these were the only traces of fatigue, the rest of the face looked sculptured, there were no traces of puffiness and not a black-head or a blemish in sight. He was very handsome, but quite old, perhaps twenty even. He had made a great effort to look untidy.

'D'you always stare like that?'

'Oh, I'm sorry, I just hadn't got a chance to look at you before. Nobody said anything to me about you. I never listen to those things anyway. I like to make up me own mind', said Margaret as she twitched her itching nose.

'Well, now you've seen me, how about this dance?'

Margaret surrendered to the hands without comment, her foot throbbed with pain and she tried to forget it by listening more intently to the music. As the tango reversed them, she felt her left ear-ring being dislodged, she put up her hand in mild panic only to touch her partner's lips before they finally parted on her tiny neck.

'Oh, oh, I thought I was losing my ear-ring.'

'What's your name? I'm Frank, Frank Dodge.'

'I'm Margaret, Margaret Thompson, at least I think I am.'

She could say no more as she received her first real kiss at that instant. She had not known that you tasted the other person, nor that it made you feel funny – she now knew that she quite liked the taste and definitely liked the feeling.

There was a double action film showing at the 'Rex' cinema, the first feature a 'cowboy', the second feature a 'gangster'. The performers might just as well have changed their clothes for each film for only costume and setting provided any differences, or contrasts. Light September drizzle fell from the skies and several people sheltered under the picture-house awning awaiting their mid-week date. Frank Dodge chose to stand outside the shelter. He wore no rain-coat. He had turned up the collar of his brown suit and had propped himself against one of the four colonnades which supported the fire escape. He watched Margaret arrive and took some pleasure in seeing her anxiety as she searched the faces outside the cinema. She climbed the steps and entered the foyer, she seemed to be in a hurry, she couldn't wait to see him again. He crossed one leg over the other and remained still; to emphasise his studied nonchalance he lit a cigarette.

Margaret quibbled over the price of a bag of liquorice allsorts with the sales lady in the foyer until finally the lady turned her metallic-blonde head away to greet a less demanding customer. Defeated, Margaret turned in indignation. She saw him standing there. His silhouette obscured the poster attached to the colonnade, a haze of smoke surrounded his face and above his head was written 'starring'. He must have been waiting in the rain for her. In the three weeks that they had known

25

each other, it was usually him that was late. This fact dissolved in the warm damp air as Margaret clopped down the steps towards him, she always felt excited just before each meeting, but now she felt tender too; it was with this mixture of pleasant guilt and excitement that she greeted him.

'Look, you're getting yourself wet standing here.' Margaret attached herself to the damp suit.

'I'm all right, come on we'll sit upstairs in the balcony.'

Frank hurried her to the cash desk. Her concern embarrassed him. She took it all a step further as they climbed into their seats in the back row of the cinema.

'You need someone to look after you.'

She said this to many people throughout her life, probably hoping that the statement might at some stage be personally applied to her. In answer, Frank hauled her across his seat, she left her gloves and bag on her own seat in case anyone should think it was vacant as she always liked to stand for the National Anthem at the end; it would be awkward when the lights went up if she didn't have a seat. Margaret managed to see the title of the film and lists of people who helped make the piece, she saw a man on a white horse disappear behind some rocks, and a man on a black horse with four other men chasing after him. The man on the black horse had a moustache, so he was bad and the one on the white horse seemed to have to get somewhere to help someone, so he was good. This was as much as she could glean from the film as Frank (like all the other men on the back row) gave his partner little opportunity to view the screen.

Like most of the other girls on the back row, Margaret legislated that Frank's hands could go anywhere as long as the area between her belly button and thighs were left untouched. This still left quite a lot of territory to explore in between the short intervals when they both emerged for brief gasps of air and a glance at the horses.

26

'I need you, touch me', groaned Frank.

He had never talked like this before and more as an act of compassion than lust, Margaret threw all social strictures aside. This seemed to increase Frank's distress rather than alleviate it and Margaret was glad when the lights went up for the interval and the organ played the Cuckoo Waltz.

'Shall I get the ice-creams, or would you like an orange drink instead?'

Margaret stood up and straightened her dress and folded her pink plastic mac carefully placing it under her seat. Frank looked most discomforted.

'Nothing for me, I'll get you one. Neapolitan?'

He rose to stand and quickly sat down again.

'You'd better get them, go on, I'll have a chocolate one.'

By the time Margaret had returned, the second feature had started and a leisurely ten minutes was spent eating and viewing.

Another fifteen minutes passed by and Margaret was a little worried as she was still sitting on her own seat.

'Are you all right?' she asked.

'Fine, like a fag?' Frank lit his and took one out for her.

'Oh, you know I don't smoke, well perhaps just one.' She still felt guilty.

'That's it, only hold the smoke in longer, now breathe it out, slowly, that's it.'

Margaret enjoyed the tutoring more than the cigarette and was relieved when the exercise was complete. Yet even after the cigarettes were finished she remained in her own seat. Frank's arm was around her, but she was able to see all of the gangster film without so much as one kiss. The arm proffered some comfort, but not enough. Occasionally she would squeeze his hand and press against him during tenser moments of the film. These were the first sexual advances that she had ever made and as she stood for the Queen at the end, she wondered if girls were supposed to do such things.

It had stopped raining and the air was warm and fresh. They walked down towards the bus-stop only to see the bus moving away still leaving a large residue of would-be travellers waiting behind. They agreed to walk home without any discussion, the silence was compatible. If they walked through the fields the journey would be halved and Margaret enjoyed climbing the stiles. There were seven in all. Each stile meant a gap in the hedgerows which divided pasture, wheat and barley. As they climbed and clambered over the stiles they laughed about nothing at all. It must have been the fourth or fifth stile that Frank slipped on. He tried to leap over it using only one hand as support on the bar. Margaret watched from the other side as the hand slipped along the wet bar and Frank's body danced in the air before it crashed on to the wooden foot stave on the other side. He lay quite still until she came to him and held his head to her.

'Are you all right?'

She kissed his forehead as she spoke and brushed his ears with her nose. He rose quietly and guided her to the side of the hedgerow. She watched him break down the bracken with his feet, she let him take off her mac and lay it down over the wet bramble and broken fox-gloves. The pain was still in his face as it lowered towards her. No admonitions were delivered as he pulled and tugged at her clothes and then without a word, he transferred his pain to her. It was only then that she cried out a little but the cry died in the air and barely reached the body above her.

She could see him waiting at the stile. He had left her immediately afterwards in a great hurry to leave the spot where they had lain, abolishing its reality by quick flight. In the rush to get away she had forgotten her raincoat. He had left her to collect it alone. For some reason she thought it might not be there. She shook the wetness away from it and put it on. Still numb she began to tidy the hedgerow folding back the broken fox-gloves and rearranging the crushed bramble.

'Come on Margaret', he called and that was all he said to her, apart from 'I'll see you then', before she turned the corner of Tree Tops Avenue.

'Is that you Margaret, it's twenty to twelve, we're all in bed' – Cora's voice pierced the night before the door was closed behind her.

'Yes, it's me, I missed the last bus, I had to walk it.' Amazed at her over-composure, Margaret continued, 'I won't be long in coming up, I'll just clean my shoes first.'

'Don't burn the light then, love, you know we're not made of money.' Len's flat whining voice joined the chorus.

Margaret cleaned her teeth with extra attention and gargled and spat the water out into the bowl.

'If that was love, if that was love, they could keep it.'

She gave her mouth another rinse before retiring.

Frank Dodge's letter which arrived three weeks later completed the disinfection.

Army Catering Corps.,
Section 7, Aldershot.

Dear Margaret,

As you can see, I have joined the Terras. I suppose lots of people in Runnock have told you anyway as news gets round quick in Runnock. I want to see a bit of the world and I weren't going to see much of it if I were down the pit, so I joined up. Me Mam thought it weren't a bad idea and the old man didn't seem to mind.

I don't know when I'm to be home again so won't make any promises. As you can see, I'm not much of a letter writer so don't bother to answer. Please don't call round our house after me because you know now I won't be there. Get yourself another bloke – I know I wasn't the first you'd had because some of the lads said they'd been out with you. I've left Runnock now and my Mam don't want any trouble.

All the best
Frank.

29

'Is it from one of your pen-friends that you wrote to while you were at school?'

As Cora had examined the post-mark of the letter, she knew that a positive response would mean a lie. She had a nice way of setting her snares. Fortunately, Margaret was more intelligent than her new guardian, she folded the letter, took a sip of morning tea and shook her head.

'It's from Frank Dodge.'

'What's he doing down Ald. . . ., what's he doing writing letters to you? Oh, our Margaret, I hope you're not gadding round with the likes of him. He's a real townie, his Dad was the same. . . .'

'He has joined the Territorial Army; he is serving Her Majesty the Queen and he might have to go to Singapore or the Middle East. He might like a letter from me now and again to cheer him up.'

Margaret had taken her cup to the draining board as she spoke. Patriotism often figured in Margaret's defence strategies.

'Oh, well, we'd best be off then, Margaret, we don't want to be late.'

It wasn't until she sat on the top of the bus that the tears came. She opened the window a little and watched the fragments of torn letter fly into the air as she released them.

'Good people of Runnock Chase, the last and yet first of you. . . .'

'Margaret, you are forgetting the long "a". The feeling is there my dear, but don't let it slaughter your sounds.'

Lena Menton, LCMA, LDAF, MRLA, teacher of drama and speech, pushed her green fly-away spectacles on to the top of her head to make a coronet.

'Try again dear, but remember the l a a a st d a a a nce, the l a a st d a a nce, the long "a" is not for the tango, but the d a a a nce. Yes, that's better, attend to posture my love, don't curve round shoulders back, but keep your chin in, tucked well in, it's not the best of your features, use your eyes more, and remember what I have said about breathing.'

Lena remembered it for her aloud.

'Intercostal diaphragmatic, the air goes up through the nasal passages down through the wind-pipe and out through the lungs. You have lungs so there's never need for you to gulp, except for a dramatic pause.'

This was the first class of its kind ever presented in Runnock. It was held on Saturday mornings at the Mining College. It was listed under leisure amenities and fourteen people had attended for just over a year. All but two belonged to local amateur dramatic societies.

'Adrian darling, could you listen to Margaret's pieces and she listen to yours. Then come back and let me know what you have said about one another, and if you see that register man Lawton coming up the drive, come and let me know. Go and practise in the top hall – stand near the window.'

Attendances had been dropping and Mr Lawton visited at the Council's expense to report back whether or not this particular leisure pursuit was worth the £3 per session invested in Lena's salary. Lena had no feeling for him or for that matter for any of the class except for Adrian and Margaret. She often informed them of this, at quiet moments, usually when they were carrying her shopping bags for her.

'Have nothing to do with St Mark's Dramatic Society, it's your soul they're after not your talent. Your style, your essence will be ruined if you tread Church Hall Boards; the Runnock Players my dears, they are worse, just front runners for the Establishment with their piddly farces. Think of Edith, Sybil, Peggy, Socialists all of them. An artist belongs to the people, never forget that. Margaret, you carry the cabbage, my love, Adrian, hold the other handle of the bag. If it weren't for you two, I am sure I would leave Runnock.' ˙

'But where would you go, Mrs Menton?'

'Oh, away, with a man somewhere.'

These confidences bound Margaret and Adrian to Lena and although they were longing to appear in a thriller or a piddly-farce they never succumbed to the overtures made to them by either the dramatic side of the Church or the Conservative Party.

32

Adrian stood at the window. He wore a bottle green suit, green suede shoes and white shirt and a yellow tie. He was tall and thin with green eyes, he said that they were hazel eyes, and he said that his features were sensitive and he said that he would not age because of this. He was an expert on information about himself. Margaret thought that he looked like a daffodil standing at the window swaying to the rhythm of the words as they fell from his full red lips.

'I think you move your hands too much, and when you're not moving them don't let them hang as though your wrists were broken.'

Their friendship was based on objectivity unusual in adolescence.

Adrian was not injured by Margaret's observations.

'Do you want to do your bits now? Here look, Margo.'

He motioned her to the window before she could answer his question.

'It's the Labour Party Parade. I used to win all of them', said Margaret flatly. 'They always have them in August – were you never in one?'

'No, I did all my dressing up at home and going to the Grammar School, I didn't have time to know what was going on in Runnock. I seem to have spent all my life travelling to school, that was a waste of time, one "O" Level in English and a lot of Latin verbs that I want to forget.'

He sat on the window ledge.

'But that was because you were idle, not because you weren't clever. You've told me about lots of things we never learned at Lime Pit Lane School. The story you told me last night by that woman who wrote using a man's name, it was. . . .'

'L a a a st night Margo, l a a a a st night, not last. I didn't learn that at school, I found it for myself. It's better finding out for yourself, those pieces I did for RADA I found for myself. I shan't miss Runnock – perhaps me mother, and you a bit.'

He placed his hand on her head and she took it and held it.

'It won't be the same when you are gone. We are good friends, aren't we?'

He stood and linked arms with her and the two of them stood at the window. It was unusual for them to touch each other in private. They had never kissed. Publicly they had entwined themselves around one another like runner beans and ivy. According to Cora their demonstrations of affection were the talk of Runnock and no good could come of it. Margaret had never mentioned engagement to her, yet they had been going out together for almost a year. Adrian and Margaret enjoyed fooling the fooled. Each had realised the vulnerability of the other and did their utmost to protect. Adrian's mother looked after a public house and Margaret would spend evenings helping behind the bar and talking. Sometimes she would stay the night sleeping on the put-u-up in the lounge. Other evenings, Adrian would see her home on the bus and then walk back alone. He was very courteous. It was one of these bus rides that formulated the basis of Adrian's commitment and admiration for her.

It had been a happy evening. Adrian's mother had told them a funny story about Nora; one of the barmaids who had married what she thought was a Polish migrant miner, only to find out later that he came from Newcastle and that his real name was Walter and not Vladimir.

'Not that it made much difference by the time she found out – 'cos she'd had a baby by then, and you've got so much to occupy you then that you can't be worryin' about where people come from or who they are. It don't matter as long as you are happy, duck, does it? Our Adrian can 'ave who the bloody hell he likes as long as he's glad on it, but you have to be careful, love.'

With a cautionary laugh she ambled her large, but heavily scented frame into the bar. Adrian then spent a lot of time making Margaret's face up, providing a commentary on each mask that he gave her.

34

'We'll tie your hair back for this one, and swing it round to the side.'

'Oh, it makes my jaw stick out, I'm not a boxer you know.'

'Wait, we'll make your eyes dramatic, wild, like Linda Darnell.'

'What about me mouth, my top lip has. . . .'

'Just shut it for a minute if you can. I'll put a record on for you; just relax and listen.'

In turn, she had highlighted his mouse-coloured hair at the front and a trace at the sides. The hours melted in make-up creams, dyes and fantasy and they had to leave in haste in order to catch the bus. They jumped on to the platform as the bus was leaving and with much gasping for breath and tittering, climbed the stairs. They began to make their way towards a seat at the front when Adrian stumbled and fell forward. Margaret had seen the pointed black shoe shoot into the passage-way, but it was too late to cry a warning. Adrian performed well, picked himself up without a murmur or a glance round and made his way forward with Margaret following warily behind. A group of Frank's old friends, about nine in all, occupied a section of the bus. One of the group had also contributed the black pointed shoe.

'That's a bad cold you've got, Jack.'

'A-poof! A-a-a-poof! A-a-a-poo o o o f! A a a a poof!'

Others on the bus began to snigger and chuckle. Margaret held on to Adrian's arm as the bus sped forward. He stared coldly ahead, his face had gone white and small muscles were twitching in the side of his neck. The derisive chorus grew louder and the obscene sneezing noises stung her like a horde of mosquitoes. Adrian had become rigid, whether from fear or anger Margaret could not ascertain.

'A-a-a-poof! A-a-a-poof! A-a-a-a-poof!'

The noise grew louder and without thinking Margaret rose and made her way towards it. By the time that she had reached the source of the noise, the noise itself had stopped and Margaret found herself looking at the nine youths. A few sniggers came from them, but they were more probably due to nerves than wilful provocation. Yet one of them proved bolder than the rest.

"Ad yer eyeful or 'ave yer lost yer glasses?'

He turned as he spoke and Margaret recognised the shoe that had instigated the torment. Normally she shrieked when she was angry, but for some reason her voice came out in a low hiss which matched the poise of her neck which stretched forward to give her some semblance of a boa-constrictor.

'I've not had my eyeful, I have to take a good look, because I can't believe what I see.'

She got rid of her chewing gum by spitting it out on the floor and continued her tirade.

'I feel sorry for you lot, I really do. Do you all have to meet together every night? Do you do your courtin' in groups? Or do you need to be together because you're frightened of being on your own? Don't you smile, Timmy Franklin, I knew you in Hancock Street, always squawk-arsin' for your mother – "Oh, Mam, she's hit me, Mam, Mam, Mam." Look, you lot had better sit together because nobody is going to want to sit with you. Why don't you all bloody hold hands and have done with it.'

'Oh, shurrup, shurrup, Marg, we was on'y joking.'

Others quickly joined in, anxious for a conciliation and hopeful that this reciprocal exposure might end.

'Before I get off this bus, there's something else you lot ought to know.'

She bent forward and gesticulated with her finger towards Adrian, who was still sitting bolt upright staring fixedly ahead.

'He has had me; he can go on having me whenever he likes and I'll let him. He knows what to do because he's a man and he's human. When you've found out what it's like to be both, then you all might risk separating a bit, and if you're bloody lucky, some girl might want to look after you or something. I think they'll be in for a bad time from what I can see, but I daresay there might be some fools around. I should try to

36

find one if I were you Timmy, and John Elesmore, and you Billy.'

The top of the bus was silent, except for a few uncomfortable coughs from other passengers who were busy trying to imagine that they were somewhere else. No one had looked round as interest might have meant involvement and at this juncture nobody was going to risk an encounter with this odd girl standing up on top of the bus.

'Adrian, come on, this is our stop, we don't want to miss it.'

He obeyed and walked the passage way free of hindrance or denigration. Before they descended the iron steps, Margaret struck again.

'Have you got a fag, Timmy?'

One was tossed to her and she caught it with both hands.

'Thanks, Adrian always likes a smoke afterwards. Ta-ra.'

They walked holding hands, just like five-year-olds first attending school, she began singing and asked him if he would try to sing 'second voice' with her. He broke the song half-way through.

'It was good of you to tell a lie like that. You are good, Margo. All of Runnock will talk about you now though, you know that don't you?'

'I don't care, I'm not staying here.' She had decided on this exactly on the second she spoke it. She would travel to London soon. Where she would stay and what she would do had taken no form. There would be no point in staying with Adrian gone. Not that she was following, it was just a case of things being over – almost like leaving school. One day you were singing Lord Dismiss Us and the next day He had and that was that. 'Corlen' greeted them both and Margaret averted her eyes from a grinning gnome that was sitting on the lawn. Cora had even given the plaster monstrosities names. They placed them in the garage when it snowed. Adrian stood at the gate and Margaret waited for the kiss which was always placed on the centre of her forehead.

'Margo, have you . . .' he paused. 'Margo, have you ever been with a man? I mean have you. . . .'

She cut in quickly, 'Have you?'

His silence was short. She was not interested in his suffering.

'Well look, don't ask me then. We can tell if we want to, but no asking.'

This seemed reasonable. Adrian delivered his blessing and was gone.

For years afterwards he remembered the phrase 'We can tell if we want to, but no asking.' It offered understanding without curiosity and much later he found out that when people wanted to help, they also usually wanted to know. Margaret wasn't like that. If he were ever famous or rich he would look after her, she could do whatever she liked – such was the intensity of his present state of gratitude.

'I don't know whether to take the mauve or the black.'

Lena Menton ignored the exasperated sighs of the girl behind the market stall and held up both pullovers. She turned to Margaret who had been edged away from the stall by would-be buyers. Lena held one pullover up first and then the other in sales semaphore. Margaret nodded to both signals and Lena looked puzzled.

'Take both of them, there's five shillings off if you buy two', shouted Margaret.

Lena joined her, happy about not having to decide and pleased with her purchase.

'I shall miss you, Margaret; but you do understand that I am not able to write to you. I have singled you out as the only person in Runnock who is able to respect and understand my situation and my confidence. Not a word to anyone at the class, but note the reactions when they receive my letter of resignation.

Please note the effect of one sentence on small minds and put it down as part of your training. Could you hold the vegetable bag, dear?'

Margaret took the heavier of the two bags and Lena linked arms with her.

'Training for what?' asked Margaret.

Lena looked surprised, but answered quickly, 'For life, my dear, for life.'

Lena placed her bag down when they reached the corner of the street and Margaret took this as an indication of a final farewell.

'I hope he'll be good to you, Lena, what will you do if he decides to. . . .'

'I'll manage, Margaret my love. Let's just look at one another, shall we? Then I'll go this way and you go that. I have no advice for you, only hope.'

Lena's usually resonant tones had begun to quaver. The bags of food and clothing were placed at their feet and the two women gave each other a minute of silent, respectful staring. Lena finally put forward both her hands and Margaret held them for a second. They smiled, then turned and walked away according to plan. Neither of them glanced back. Lena's progress was slow now that she was forced to carry both bags, but Margaret half ran to the outskirts of the town centre within a matter of minutes. Margaret had wondered what the content of Lena's departure performance would be like. She had expected tears from both sides, but the restraint from Lena and herself had jolted her by its sincerity. This dissolved the terrible desolation that she had experienced at the 'good-byes' of Aunt Florrie and Adrian. Even whilst walking home with her legs and arms moving she felt quite still. No. 4 Pit just rose out of the heather before her and she stopped to look at it.

There were at least fourteen coal-mines dispersed throughout Runnock and most of the male population worked down them.

It was quite possible never to see a quarter of Runnock's men because of the night shift. Their normal rest was spent in working darkness and their sleep took up the day-light. The stacks and mounds reared up in the middle of the fern and silver birch; pine-trees destined to become pit-props skirted the hills with military precision, nothing grew under these trees, all vegetation had been crushed by layer after layer of pine-needle, they were not attractive to view, but when dry, they were comfortable to sit on. Margaret sat and contemplated the huge mounds of slag and waste and watched the whirring wheels of the cage as it hauled men working miles beneath her to the surface. It was difficult to determine which of them were young or old, the grime and dust seemed to have no respect for either. They left the pit in groups of three or four. They didn't talk much – for some reason talking didn't seem necessary. It was strange, Margaret had never met a miner at the Co-op Dance. Did coal-miners dance? Lena had said that miners were the only true repertory company within the nation and, as such, they should be revered. Margaret hadn't really understood what Lena meant by this, nor had the rest of the class; but then, Lena's passionate declamations were usually delivered to the air and seemed to bear no relation to what was said before or afterwards. In this sense her departure mirrored her beliefs. She did not deem it necessary to define feelings by reason or intellect. This probably helped her to avoid a great deal of personal suffering which came her way. She had never subjected herself to compromise in any form. Her flight from Runnock involved no personal recrimination or guilt, it was a practical move.

No letters arrived from Lena, and unfortunately there was little reaction to her absence from the drama class. Mr Lawton, the superintendent, merely closed it and another class on local studies was substituted in its place. Margaret did not attend – she preferred her own assessment of her environment – and the months of July and August provided her with fresher and

41

warmer insights of her birthplace, but even these only increased her alienation and confirmed rather than delayed her eventual departure.

The Co-op Dance held no curiosity or wonder now, the cinema visitations were selective not routine, and Cora and Len had cause to complain.

'A girl your age shouldn't be stuck at home every evening. What do you do up there?'

'I read.' Margaret paid her board and lodging. This did not include conversation with Len or Cora. If this had been the case she would have demanded a reduction in rent. It was true her evenings were spent more in her room but she was not unhappy. The week-ends provided her with a new source of interest which had as its centre the countryside itself. Her long walks took her along canals, built to carry the coal, and to dark deep watery pools, testaments to deserted 'Jack' pits or gravel excavations. Grass camouflaged these man-made haunts and iris and bull-rush gave added decoration.

'Yes – but I don't want yer talkin' or fidgetin' about, just stay where you are.'

The fisherman spoke gruffly without looking round. He held his rod in his left hand and without changing its position he stretched down and lifted a handful of maggots from his bait-tin, he tossed them on the air and they swirled on the water before sinking around the float which bobbed ten yards from the bank of the canal. Margaret did as she was told and sat alongside the long pink willow herb that flecked the bank. She watched the last of the maggots squirm beneath the surface of the water and disappear. Five minutes passed by, but it seemed longer to her. The flock from the willow herb was beginning to choke her nostrils as it caught the afternoon breeze.

'Do you sit here long before anything happens?'

There was no answer so she spoke louder but kept her inquisition polite.

'You might do better with a big net. If there were two of you, perhaps you could dredge the canal with it. Like they dredge the sea.'

The answer came quick and sharp.

'Shu-rr-up. Shu-rr-up – sit still or I'll dredge you. Now shurrup and look at the float, that's the red thing floating out there – just watch it.'

It began to bob up and down in the water and then commenced swerving across the canal as though it were possessed. Margaret forgot the willow herb now, captive to this magic. The rod jerked and Margaret found herself peering over the edge of the canal as the fish flopped and floundered in the shallow water.

'Pass the landing net, love; it's that long pole thing with the triangle stuck on the end of it, place it under the fish, that's it, don't bash him on the side.'

She lifted the fish out of the water and placed it on the bank. Its mouth seemed large in comparison to its seven-inch body. The fish gasped as it lay on the damp cloth. Margaret noted its pale green scales and the three or four olive green strips which circled its width. One long spiky fin stretched almost from its head to its tail. The fisherman handled it with care, the hook was removed from the mouth quickly, deftly, and Margaret was proffered a closer look.

'It's like a shark with that thing on its back. You would never think that these would live in the canal, would you?'

The man placed the fish carefully back in the shallows. It looked smaller now, it turned twice as if to relish its freedom and then bolted only to leave a cloud of muddied water behind.

'Do you always put them back then?'

'Ah, I do. If I took all of 'em out I caught, there'd be none left in the cut.'

He folded his raincoat.

'Sit yourself on this if you're staying. There'll be more perch to be had this afternoon. That's what that fish was, duck; a perch. They're brave fish, no mucking about with them. They never play with the bait, they know what they want and get it.'

He wiped his hands on the cloth, removed his cap from his head and cast his line into the water. She sat at his feet, curled in his raincoat like some lost kitten. He had only looked at her twice and on both times orders had been given. He was dark haired with large brown eyes. His mouth was full and there was a small space between his two front teeth. If he hadn't been sitting on the canal bank in Runnock he might have been a very pale Italian. Margaret was so intent on placing him on the Ponte Vecchio that she was unable to retrieve the tin of maggots which her extended foot had kicked into the canal. Desperately she lunged forward as it rolled over the grey bank only to send it further into the water with her outstretched hand.

'Bloody 'ell, what are you doin'? Now all me bait's gone. It's no good just sittin' there lookin' and starin'. It's gone, the bait's gone.'

His statement was so complete, but what could she do but stare? It wouldn't be right to say sorry because it just wouldn't cover what she felt, crying might have helped, but she couldn't feel any tears on her face.

'Worms 'll do, red worms, pull some of those clods up and bring me three or four. You'll find the best ones near the cow-flops. I'll manage with these maggots on the hook till you get back.'

'Worms?'

He nodded his head. It was a funny way to be spending a Saturday evening pulling up clods of earth and prodding round cow-shit thought Margaret, but the four red worms writhing in her palm were none the less delivered in five minutes of ordering.

'Good girl', he said.

Four more perch were caught and returned before they left and during these two hours he had not spoken but he smiled twice. Slowly each time. There were no more orders. She folded and packed his haversack as he dismembered his rod. He would not let her carry anything, everything balanced on his back. As they descended the bank of the canal, he took her arm, but did not release it even after they had reached the lane. She felt a bit like one of the perch, dangling like some marionette from his arm.

'I'm twenty-two, on the face at twos', he said.

'I'm nearly eighteen, I'm a. . . .' She paused. The lane led under an aqueduct and a railway bridge. The two hundred yards ahead were neither darkness nor twilight and something had swooped near her head. Drops of water plopped on to the pavement from the leaking arch and she discerned more shapes swishing about in the oncoming gloom.

'Can we go another way back?'

'It's only bats, they won't hurt yer, we used to catch them. All you do is spread an old net curtain across, they get stuck in them. They're funny little things, no harm in them, no harm in 'em at all.'

Margaret might have been reassured if she had not witnessed two bats squeaking in ecstasy over their copulation. She turned towards him for protection. Both his arms gripped her now, the rod fell to the floor. He kissed her long and hard, stroked her head gently and led her dazed into the early evening of the open lane. He walked her home, but there were no more embraces. She felt badly about the bats now and was irked that they had frightened her. What was all right for people ought to be all right for bats, she wouldn't be frightened of them again ever.

'I'll be there on Tuesday, the same place if you're around, duck', was all he said.

'Good Lord, Margaret, look at the state of your shoes. Don't bring them in with you, leave them in the hall, they'll ruin the tufted carpet and you know how upset Len will get. Where've you been to get in that state?'

As usual Margaret was prepared for Cora who stood swathed in a pink nylon housecoat, her face taut with irritation.

'Walking, I've been walking.'

Margaret stepped out of her shoes and walked into the kitchen.

'At this hour? It's half past nine.'

'It's cheaper than dancing, more comfortable too.'

Margaret scraped the mud from her shoes and emptied it into the bin.

'We've eaten; you could have something on toast, there's beans or pilchards.'

Cora had given up the interrogation she always lost. She picked up her knitting. There was some satisfaction in offering beans and pilchards. It had meant more ham for her and Len. They always had ham on a Saturday. An odd smell rose and swirled about Margaret and she peered about the kitchen to detect its source. The sink breathed bottled pine and the rubbish bin was clean save for mud. She brushed her hair from her face. It was stronger now. Her hands. She sniffed again, they smelt of fish scales, cow-flop, earth and red worms. It was quite new to her and she did not find it unpleasant. Nevertheless, she washed them well before going up to her room. Perhaps it was the smell that dictated the letter to Adrian.

27 Tree Tops Avenue,
Runnock.
July.

My Dear Adrian,

I always enjoy your letters and I am missing you as much as you are missing me. I think I am anyway. Why are there coffee houses all over London? Do people drink it all the time? It seems a funny thing to do and I'm surprised to hear that the one you work in is open until two in the morning. The fountain sounds lovely, I've never heard of one being inside a cafe before. Your friend Andre sounds very nice. Is he a dentist in France or in London? By the time this letter gets to you your audition for Swansea will be settled. All the big stars began in repertory companies, I'm so glad for you Adrian. I know they will let you join

46

the company. There must be lots of parts for young people –
like footmen and stewards and people like that.

I won't be coming down to London in August after all;
there's nothing stopping me coming, and I will come, but I
want the Summer time here. I've never seen it until this
year or you could say I've never noticed it. For some reason
I'm looking at everything now, I don't suppose you've
watched clouds of gnats, or ever seen a bat. Neither had I
until tonight. At the moment, Runnock is very still or it
seems as though it is and I am enjoying being inside it. Do
you know at times it feels as though I'm dreaming. I wish
you were here to share it all with me. This kind of Summer
can't last. I'll see you in London or Swansea – wherever –
it will be good.

Fondest love Margo   XX

P.S. I am thinking of taking up fishing. Do you know any
Italians?

Margaret was settled in bed quickly and her thoughts were
based not on the past or future, but the present. This offered
her no anxieties or concern, the present appeared simple and
uncluttered, she was developing an appetite for it. Under this
warm panoply of rural duplicity she slept soundly.

There were 612 houses on the Renton Green Estate. Its boundaries were sharply defined. One was the main road to Runnock, another was Renton No. 2 Pit. The railway finally separated its eastern end from the tracts of gravel excavations and heather. It was known as Renton Village and the bus service to Runnock was on the hour until nine p.m. After such time the two mile walk to the town centre had to be undertaken by any inhabitant seeking a busier scene. Most men and women over twenty-three rarely had cause to walk far. All the men worked in Renton Colliery, all the houses belonged to Renton Colliery and what leisure existed apart from the countryside, was provided by Renton Colliery Working Men's Club. Girls had two choices, they could either leave Renton Green or marry. Most of them chose the latter. Curtains and numbers were the only items which distinguished one house from another. The grey acres of pebble-dash had not quite killed all creativity. The gardens bore no such uniformity. Some were barren and overgrown, covered with pot-holes and weeds, others were all rabbit hutches, pigeon pens and green-houses. They bulged with vegetables. Occasionally, one would come across one rampant with flowers, ill-planned but triumphant in growth and colour. Renton Green was the nearest that one could ever get to a very progressive prison.

'Our Richard 'as bin good to me, never a bit of trouble.' Mrs Cartwright tightened the knot on her pinafore and turned to straighten a chalk doll on the side-board which was already straight.

'He bought me this; it's a "shy girl", oh, yes he's a good boy.'

He is a man now, thought Margaret. This was her second visit to Richard Cartwright's home. The small room seemed crowded. It might have been the awkward brown three-piece suite or the four women which gave it this feeling. The photo-graphs that stared from every wall and shelf did not help at all. Linda and Maureen, his two older sisters, chewed sponge cake as Mother talked.

'I'm never on me own, our Linda lives opposite and our Maureen is just round the back and they call round every day – don't yer, ducks?'

Linda and Maureen smiled smugly and continued to chew. Mrs Cartwright continued the daily family eulogy placing her children sweetly and permanently in debt to her for bearing them.

'I had to rear them on me own, it was 'ard then. When the telegram came they weren't much more than babies. It was the only telegram I'd ever 'ad. My Alf killed in Sicily.'

Maureen and Linda had heard the story before, but waited like children anticipating the re-telling, avid to relish the familiar as though it were Cinderella or Red Riding Hood.

'He needn't 'ave left the pit, miners didn't have to go and fight. I still blame him for leaving. I dunno' what entered his head. Anyway, I thought he'd be safe in a tank, great big iron things you know. It didn't help him none.'

She shook her head.

'No it didn't help him at all. Burned.'

In spite of herself and the torpor of the afternoon, Margaret was startled

'Oh, I'm sorry.'

Mrs Cartwright was pleased with the reaction, she had told the story so many times and it never failed her.

'Yes, burned, scorched to a cinder by a flame-gun, probably not a hair of his head left. Him buried over there and me left with all the kids. They've bin golden to me though, more than made up for his leavin' me. His picture was in the *Runnock Star* you know. They say our Richard looks like 'im but I can't tell now. It was such a long time ago and you forget, don't yer? I never thought our Richard would be interested in girls, you're 'is first one yer know. He's a quiet lad, never a bit of trouble and he still turns up his bag on a Friday. I told 'im he could pay board if he liked, but he said to leave things as they was. It's not as though he is lodging here is it? After all, duck, I am his Mother.'

'I'll give him a hand with the pigeons.' Margaret had to get out of the room quickly, she did not wait for any more words, but she did hear Linda say, 'What's a girl want with pigeons?'

'It's him she wants, not the birds', said Maureen, her mouth half-full of cake, but by this time Margaret was half-way down the garden path.

'Come on then, come on then, come on then, you're a beauty. Come on then, come on.'

Margaret stopped a short distance from the pen. Richard was calling the pigeons, not her. He was standing on a raised platform at the front of the pen scattering corn seeds as he cajoled the birds from sky to home. They flew so close to one another it was strange that the changes in formation caused no collision. Margaret raised her hand to shield her eyes as the birds skirmished the pen and then rose and encircled the air once more.

'Come up on the platform, you can see better from here.'

She had waited for the invitation. He was always gentle and crude. No not crude, direct would be better. Margaret looked at him, he smiled at her.

'Are yer comin' up 'ere, "dreamy Lil", or stayin' down there?'

'Oh, I'm coming up.'

The pigeons zoomed towards the pen. Margaret hadn't expected thirty birds could make so much noise.

'The little blue hen, see her? She's the leader.'

Richard placed his hand on Margaret's shoulder and traced the line of flight with his other outstretched hand.

'Do they always come back? You'd think they'd just fly away with all that space, they could fly away couldn't they?'

'They could, ah p'raps they could, but they don't. They allus come in 'cos they know where their bread's buttered. Some of 'em are a bit slow at the moment 'cos they're nigh on being broody.'

This puzzled Margaret, she hadn't thought of pigeons as being particularly sensitive creatures before.

'Do they get upset then?' she enquired.

'Upset, what do yer mean upset? No I wouldn't let them get upset, broody is when they're comin' on to lay, it's when the cocks start all their bother and the hens don't mind. 'Ere come and look.'

He motioned her to the inside of the pen. It was scrupulously clean save for one or two discarded feathers. Margaret stooped and picked one up.

'It's blue, this feather's blue', she said.

'See, the hens are beginning to nest, that's what the piles of straw and feathers are all about, gettin' ready for layin' ', he said placing the bag of corn on the platform and sitting on the edge.

'You catch the fish and put them back, and you look after birds who are free to go if they want. But they don't, and I can't say I blame them.'

Margaret brushed his ear with the feather as she spoke. He laughed and shook his head.

'Give over, give over doing that.'

She continued and he laughed more.

'I warned yer, don't say I didn't warn yer.'

He grabbed her shoulders and pulled her down on to the platform.

'I'll lock yer in the pen if yer don't behave yerself.'

He struggled to take the feather from her hand and both laughingly rolled into the pen. She kissed him on the space of neck between the ear and the shoulder and he stroked her in many places.

'Oh, Richard, oh, Richard.'

'What's the matter, duck?' he murmured.

'Nothing, nothing really, only I think I've gone broody. . . .'

His breathing had gradually become quieter, she felt as though both of them had been flying. He made no move away from her but placed his head on her small breasts.

'Thank you, my love', said Richard.

'Thank you, my love', said Margaret.

'The marks on your back, they're not tattoos are they?' she asked.

'No, I don't want any needles in me. I'm pretty enough without coloured pictures. Them are scars.'

'Scars? But they're blue.'

'Pit scars all of 'em.'

He kissed her belly.

'Just like the pigeons', she said.

He sat up. 'Yer what?'

'The scars, they are blue, the same as the pigeons.'

He laughed and drew her to him.

'You're a funny one, I don't know what I'm going to do with yer, do I?'

He answered his own question in the simplest way.

Neither of them heard the pigeons cooing as they pecked corn from the platform, nor were they aware of Mrs Cartwright who had quietly closed the pen door on them.

'There's a house 'ull soon be empty in Renton Lane, next to the off-licence, it's a ten minute walk away from me mother. Its coal-board and the gaffer says it 'ud be mine if I was married, 'Ow about it?'

Margaret was shocked with the proposal. The thought of Renton Green terrified her, yet Richard Cartwright seemed more real than anyone she had ever encountered before. On the other hand, her experience was limited.

'What's up?' he asked.

'Are you sure you love me then?'

'I couldn't touch you like I do if I didn't, could I?'

Margaret had not answered any of his questions. She liked being with him. In some ways he seemed separate from everything. She valued him. He had made her happy in a very quiet way. She smiled as she thought about it all.

'Did you put the kettle on, Margaret? It's twenty past ten, they've had a busy morning so far. Mr Barraclough has bought us all doughnuts for tea break.'

Miss Wilmot beamed and placed more house contract letters on her desk. The early morning October rain had stopped, but the shower had left the War Memorial glistening. She didn't look at it quite so much now. She tore bits from her doughnut because she liked to eat the bit with the raspberry jam in last of all. A girl she was at school with squirted the jam in with a pointed thing. Margaret wondered what a jam doughnut squirter thought about. She was down to the last fragment before she realised that her doughnut was barren. She swallowed it down with a gulp of tea feeling distinctly cheated. There were few complaints about her work. She had become an efficient typist, probably faster than Miss Wilmot. The work did not tax her as she could type in the same way as most women could knit. The morning had almost click-clacked away before the commotion started.

'But you can't come in here without an appointment, this is a solicitors' office, not the market.'

Miss Wilmot was almost shouting. The opening of the office door coincided with the reply which was almost a shriek.

'I 'ave to see Miss Davis, I 'ave to see Margaret Davis, me Mam gave me the address.'

Linda Cartwright stood inside the office. Margaret moved towards her and Linda burst into tears. Miss Wilmot remained unmoved.

'This won't do, not in here, please.'

Linda ignored her lack of concern.

'It's Richard, there's been an accident, something at the pit', her voice rose as she blubbered on.

'Me Mam said to fetch yer, she gave the address, p'haps I've done wrong coming in like this.' She began to sob as much with embarrassment as with fear. Margaret put on her coat.

'You did right, duck, you did right coming for me.'

Here she was talking as though she were a Cartwright.

'My dear, time off is only granted for a bereavement; a whole day for Mother or Father and a half-day for brother or sister. Does this man er, is he your next of kin?'

Miss Wilmot moved to the door space.

'Oh, he's not dead', wailed Linda.

Margaret had picked up her bag.

'Excuse me, Miss Wilmot, I must leave now. I have no relatives, no father, no mother, nor sister nor brother. By my reckoning, this means I can go into mourning for all of them, which gives me two days clear.'

'Well I don't know what Mr Barraclough is going to say, I've never heard such goings on in all the years that I have been here.'

Her two string pearl necklace snapped as she tugged at it in indignation.

'Come on, Linda, we can catch the twelve o'clock bus if we rush.'

The pearls crunched beneath their feet as they left.

'You go inside with Maureen, Linda. Our Margaret 'ull stay 'ere with me.'

Mrs Cartwright sat a few yards from the shaft along with two other women whose expressions were blank, there was little or no conversation between the groups. Mrs Cartwright spoke again.

'There's bin a fall, duck, a roof fall and Charlie Penfold, Mannie Hayes and our Richard are under it, or trapped the other side of it. The men are trying to clear it down there now, we must just wait 'ere, duck, it's all we can do.'

Margaret sat on the pit-prop next to her and they linked hands.

'I knew you'd come. Yer a funny thing, but I knew you'd come. I know what our Richard sees in yer. I knew you'd come.'

'How long have they been. . . . ?'

56

'Since ten o'clock this morning. You must wait, duck.'
Mrs Cartwright stroked her hand.

'But that's five hours, I mean if they are under the coal,
they'll be. . . .'

'No, no, if they can pump some air through, they can last
for days. There's some good men down there routing for 'em,
if they can be got out they'll be got.'

Margaret understood Lena's talk of miners as she listened
to Mrs Cartwright. The stubborn optimism seemed to spring
from her dull grey hair. Margaret moved closer to her and she
did not object. By seven in the evening the numbers of people
at the pit-head had increased and four hours later, there was
not a soul in Renton Green that was not waiting. The families
sat in groups wrapped with blankets, a respectful distance was
kept from the three affected families. They sat apart whilst the
others waited with them in tribal sympathy. A well dressed
young woman approached Margaret.

'I'm from the press.'

'Sod off, go on sod off', said Mrs Cartwright.

Margaret's back ached, it might help to walk about a
little, but no one else was moving and soon she entered the
ritual of stillness and waiting. There were no glances at the
darkened sky or her watch, no thought for the cold, nor the
fine rain. It was as though all feelings and thoughts had been
scooped away and buried, yet there was nothing ghost-like
about the people of Renton Green as they sat and waited.

At three in the morning the wheels of the iron cage began to
whir and simultaneously the colliery manager shook his head
very slowly to the almost silent crowd. A whisper passed
through it just louder than the evening breeze. This was followed by silence which was only broken by the creaking
wheels of the cage. It was not until the three shattered bodies
were carried out by twelve exhausted men that the stillness
was broken.

'Oh my Christ in 'eaven.'

The cry did not come from the immediate bereaved, but from a voice in the crowd. There was no hysteria, the single cry had summarised all collective feelings. The sobbing began. Mrs Cartwright stood and led Margaret by the arm.

'They were under it; not trapped, must 'ave bin a ton or more, they're broken up, all of 'em. It's bad, it's a bad business. Ah'm sorry duck.'

The elderly miner could say no more.

'This one's our Richard, I know his boots.'

Mrs Cartwright knelt down and held the head and blanket-covered shoulders of the broken corpse in her lap. An arm flopped from the blanket and Margaret stooped and held the outstretched hand, a trickle of blood and dust moistened her palm.

'Why?' was all that came from her mouth and Mrs Cartwright could give no answer. At this instant, a blinding flash of light illuminated the inert trio, a voice spoke.

'Have you any comment? I suppose you are this man's mother, I am from the pre. . . .'

Mrs Cartwright answered swiftly with a forceful slap. There were no more questions. Three older women came up and seemed to be offering some kind of service but Mrs Cartwright shook her head. Eventually she stood.

'No, I'll wash him meself, 'es my son, I'm 'is Mother. I 'ad 'im and I'll wash an bury 'im.'

Margaret nodded her head in support and it was recognised.

'Margaret 'ere, she's 'is girl, a lovely girl she is, our Richard thought the world of her, she'll help me.'

They talked as they worked on the naked body washing away the blood and erasing every speck of pit-dust visible.

'You 'ad no family of yer own did yer, love? I mean no Mam and Dad. I knew yer Mam yer know.'

Mrs Cartwright spoke hesitantly.

'I liked 'er, she was from Little Hayes, a pretty thing, nice like you. She was in service yer know, in Birmingham. She had a bad time. Work was short and money hard to get then. She 'ad you very late on. She'd be much older than me now.'

Margaret bathed the feet with warm water. She emulated Mrs Cartwright and substituted industry for grief, activity for shock. She let Mrs Cartwright talk as her own throat seemed to have become blocked.

'Pull those curtains a bit closer to, just while I clean 'im here, there that's it, now a clean handkerchief and I'll tie his jaw. I'll get his best blue suit out and clean shirt – we'll 'ave 'im lovely again.'

Margaret found her voice.

'Could he have his fishing clothes, the corduroys and the zipper jacket and the raincoat, I think. . . .'

'Yes, of course 'e can, love, course 'e can, you're right that's what 'e liked best.'

They dressed the body carefully ignoring the twisted frame and splayed legs. Touching it had helped them both.

'You'd better stay 'ere tonight, though there 'ain't much of it left. You know, duck, there'ull always be a home here for yer if want it.'

Margaret climbed into Mrs Cartwright's huge double bed and lay in the arms of the older woman.

'Our Richard 'ad yer, didn't 'e?'

'Yes he did.'

''E loved yer then, duck, and I'm glad 'e did, glad fer him not to have missed yer.'

It was then that Margaret cried, long and harshly, it was then that Mrs Cartwright's wails began and neither of them tried to assuage each other's grief which was particular and private to them.

Margaret fingered her Armistice Day poppy. Everybody bought a red poppy in order to remember, but it was difficult to remember something you had not known. She enjoyed singing 'O Valiant Hearts' when she was at school, now she felt guilty about the enjoyment. From her singular experience, she had discovered that death in no way thrilled or moved her, it merely left her numb.

'If you take the post you can leave early, dear.'

Miss Wilmot had tried to convey such small token favours to Margaret since Richard's death. It was difficult trying to help the girl as she had gone so blank and quiet. There were three letter boxes marked, Local, Other Places, London. All of Margaret's bundle shot into the 'Local' slot.

'Ps-ss-st, ps-ss-st, ps-ss-st.' Margaret ignored the noise, she no longer felt curious about men or their calls, she half turned from the post box and then pulled the poppy from her coat and posted it in 'Other Places'.

'Margaret, Marga-r-et!' A woman wearing a shiny orange balaclava beckoned to her from the shop doorway opposite. Margaret stood still and was pleasantly surprised when the brim of the helmet was turned up. It was Lena Menton.

'Quick, come into the transport cafe, I've been waiting for you.' Lena took Margaret's arm and led her inside.

'I'm at Wolhamthorpe Technical College now.'

'Is there a drama class there? I thought it was for plumbers and architects and people like that', said Margaret.

'Well it is, dear, it is, but I am assisting the Vice-Principal so to speak, just bringing a little balance into his life. In this respect I am making an inadvertent, but not slender, contribution towards the curriculum.'

Lena removed her balaclava and pushed her glasses up on to her head signifying that the oracle could no longer be consulted on this subject. She leaned forward.

'I'm so sad for you my dear, but proud oh, so proud, of you. I saw the photograph in the *Midlander Courier*. It was like looking at the Pietà in Avignon, beautiful, beautiful', Lena murmured and sighed. 'I don't suppose you've talked to anyone about it, it is necessary to talk of these things, my dear, that's why I came.'

Margaret conceded and talked and Lena Menton guided the catharsis gently as only a truly great actress could.

Margaret felt better.

'You're my fairy Godmother, Miss Menton.'

Lena looked slightly put out at this remark.

'Friend, darling, fairy friend if you like. You can call me Lena now as our ages and experience are getting closer. Thank God that youth is not chronological.'

She rummaged in her bag.

'There, that's what I wanted to give you.' She passed Margaret a card.

'Awkward'
Models that are – different – – models that sell.
     Awkward Agency, 24 Dean Street, W.1.
     Tel. CEN 2458.
Principal, Estelle Bingham-Jones.

'She will give you work when you get to London. She is in debt to me, so take what you can. In this envelope is an accommodation address, old friends of mine in Bayswater. I shouldn't stay here in Runnock much longer.'

Margaret found herself saying, 'I'm giving a week's notice from tomorrow.'

Lena straightened her skirt as she stood, Margaret noticed a long ladder in Lena's left stocking and one of her high-heels was well past the mending stage. She left Margaret with a quick wave as she spoke to one of the bus-drivers.

'Are you the driver of the Wolhamthorpe bus? I thought I had seen you before. I know your face because it's always such a smooth journey when you're in control. Yes, I live in Wolhamthorpe, I've only recently moved there. Yes, I spent many years in India. . . .'

Lena left with the driver, extolling mysteries of the East as they passed through the door together.

Margaret opened the envelope to find an address and £10 enclosed.

'Oh, Lena', she said.

'Yer what?' A young conductor was hoping to offer some assistance.

'Sorry, I was just thinking', said Margaret as she tucked the money into her purse.

'Do yer want the Renton bus, duck?' the bus conductor was still hoping.

'Oh, no, no thank you. I am travelling, but I'll be going much further than your bus can take me.'

Eight days later she stood on platform twelve marked London/Euston, she gave in her ticket at the barrier and passed through.

'I'm here', she thought.

'I'm just starting.' She frowned. This was not quite true, surely she had more than begun already.

PART TWO

A Russian Orthodox Church was the last thing Margaret expected to find in Bayswater. She had belonged to five churches in Runnock, Church of England, Baptist, Methodist, Congregational and Primitive Methodist. She believed, but felt the need for variation. If she changed churches twice each year, then it meant that she could collect at least two attendance prizes. The books she received were not always to her liking. The one on stamp collecting from the Church of England had been part exchanged for another, but she had been well pleased with an abridged version of *Jane Eyre* from the Primitive Methodists.

'I wonder what sort of book I would have got from the Russian Orthodox.'

She placed her bags down and pondered over this as she looked at the strange dome with the tiny cross perched on top.

No. 3, Petersburgh Place, was the accommodation address that Lena had given. There was no problem in finding the street, as it ran parallel to the church, but on first appearance there didn't appear to be any houses in it. The grounds of the church seemed to take up all the two hundred yards of Petersburgh Place. She had staggered up and down it twice before she noticed a small gate in the wall on the corner of Petersburgh Place and Kiev Road. It was not numbered, but irritation and fatigue dispelled any shyness and Margaret trundled in through the gate. The house was surprisingly near the road. It was large with bits sticking out of it at the side. Concrete steps led up to the front door and this was all the house that could be seen. The walls were covered with ivy and dark brown creepers. Large trees managed to surround and touch the place as if it were a bare stage that had to be covered by ladies of the chorus.

'You were expected at two. Have you had trouble with the trains?' A very tall, distinguished looking man opened the door. He wore a dark blue suit, a white shirt and a black tie. The severity of his dress was relieved by two thick red stripes which ran down the sides of his trousers from his waist to his ankles.

'Signal trouble, I suppose?'

'No', said Margaret, but he had turned, picked up her bags and was already speaking over his shoulder.

'Sir Vivian is waiting in the library, it's this way.'

Margaret followed him past two brass herons which leered in the hall-way into a small room that looked more like a nursery as it was overrun with toy soldiers, forts and model railways. Sir Vivian sat in a space surrounded by a squad of Sepoy soldiers, a railway siding and the remains of Fort Hyderabad.

'Carry on, Wintner, carry on', he muttered as he quickly moved a platoon from behind a siding nearer to the fort. He spoke again, 'We'll need to fan out unless. . . .'

66

'Pardon me', said Margaret who was puzzled rather than alarmed.

Sir Vivian ignored her enquiry by staring intently at the battleground surrounding him, clearly he was in a permanent state of siege.

The man in red striped trousers stood and gave a little cough.

'Ahem, I'm Wintner.'

'Oh, hello Mr Wintner, pleased to meet you I'm sure.' Margaret felt a bit better now. 'I think there has been a bit of a breakdown in communication or something like that, Mr Wintner.'

He drew the dark green curtains as he spoke and switched on a tall standard lamp which cast a spotlight on Sir Vivian sprawled on the rug.

'The name is Wintner, miss, er, no 'Mr', just Wintner, if you don't mind.'

Margaret felt sorry for him.

'Oh dear, aren't you allowed to be even a 'Mr' then? I think that's terrible.'

He did not want her sentiments.

'Not terrible, miss, not terrible, just form. It's just form. Now when you answered our advertisement, you said that terms would be discussed and decided on, appertaining to experience and qualification, etcetera, etcetera. Ahem, ahem, I must admit I did h'expect to see er'm, shall we say, someone a little er'm more mature as they say.'

He stroked his short sideboards nervously. Any personalised observation was beyond his rule book. In this instance he had lapsed and was already regretting it. Margaret increased his discomfiture even further by answering him immediately.

'But I haven't answered any advertisement, I have come here for help. For accommodation', she blurted. 'I only arrived in London today from Runnock.'

Wintner seemed frozen but his jaw managed to move.

'Help, miss? Help? This is not a society here, this is a private 'ouse and there's no room for travellers here. This is all not a bit fortunate.'

He had already opened the library door in readiness for her departure.

Margaret sighed with relief.

'It was Miss Lena Menton who gave me the address. I suppose there has been some kind of mistake.'

Her words seemed to send Wintner and Sir Vivian into some kind of momentary catatonic trance. Wintner held on to the marble mantelpiece for support whilst Sir Vivian dropped a Bengal Lancer and half stood to remain transfixed in a kneeling position, not unlike one of the Runnock War Memorial figures. It was Sir Vivian who spoke first, or at least, he made the first noise. A low hissing which must have emanated from somewhere much deeper than his stomach, finally came from his throat as he twisted his heavy frame towards Wintner.

'H, h, h-h-h-Ha-r-r-y' he rasped. 'H-a-r-r-y, how could you do this to me. After all. . . .'

Wintner paid no attention to his newly discovered Christian name, in fact he ignored Sir Vivian completely. He addressed Margaret with new found reverence as though she were a saint or a creature from a star or planet.

'Yer did say Lena, love? Yer did say Lena Menton?'

Margaret now felt that she was no longer contagious and settled herself in a large armchair with sides that were higher than her head.

'Yes, she's a friend of mine. I would have told you before, but I never got the chance.'

She looked in her bag.

'Here is the address she gave me. It's this address, but there are no names on it, and nobody tried to find anything about me when I called. I've been ignored by one and made somebody else by another. I'm beginning to wonder who I am myself now.'

She had begun to cry a little.

Wintner handed Margaret a large white handkerchief.

"'Ere, blow, love, blow yer nose 'ard. Lena never married then, she kep' 'er promise. Solitary and true she said she'd be and she's still a "Miss".'

The remarks checked Margaret's tears and the handkerchief immediately lost its function. He spoke again as he closed the door.

'What a woman, gave up everything for me, she did. I don't suppose you know her address do yer?'

Sir Vivian rose tragically to his feet as though he were emerging fully clothed from the sea shallows.

'Harry, Harry, you're not leaving me, not now at the end of the campaign?'

Wintner ignored his question and looked towards Margaret.

'Miss Menton was my drama teacher and later my friend. However, she has never chosen to give me her address. She tends to prefer to remain incognito. That's what she is at the moment, in-cog-nito. I am afraid I couldn't ever help you to find her.'

Wintner bowed his head.

'I'm sorry', said Margaret.

'You sounded a bit like 'er yerself just now, you've brought her all back. She called me 'er knight and recited to me, spoke like you did just now – you don't know that recitation do yer?'

Wintner took the handkerchief and blew his nose. Margaret obliged.

'Oh, what can ail thee knight at arms,
Alone and palely loitering.'

'Say that bit again, I like that', said Wintner.

'Alone and palely loitering . . .', Sir Vivian roared interruption.

'Harry, Harry, I beg of you. . . .'

'Shut up, shut up', snapped Wintner.

'The sedge hath withered. . . .'

Margaret's words dried in the air as the library door was

thrust back with a bang. Wintner stood to attention and Sir Vivian said, 'My dear.'

Margaret stood to greet a woman who looked as though she had come to do the cleaning. Her hair was tied in a polka-dot turban and a few curls dribbled on to her wide brow. She was heavily rouged and the pillar-box red mouth almost overtook her nose and chin, yet she had the dedicated look of a war-time munitions factory worker. Wintner whispered to Margaret.

'Ahem, Lady Hilda, this is Miss Davis, Miss Margaret Davis.'

Lady Hilda smiled and Margaret heard a distinct click almost as if fingers were being snapped. The smile was followed by a nod in Margaret's direction. Lady Hilda spoke.

'A sherry, Wintner. A small sherry.'

The words were more of a plea than a request.

'It's a little late for sherry now, madam. Would you like tea in your room before dinner?'

'A brandy then? I hate tea, before or after dinner, I dislike tea at any time.'

She addressed Margaret.

'Do you like tea, dear?'

'Yes, I love it.'

'Good, then Wintner can make you some and you can join me later. There I've pleased both of you, the only person not satisfied is me.'

Lady Hilda left the room by delivering a noisy smile from the red-gashed mouth and approached the large stairway in the hall as if she were negotiating long distances on board ship in a stormy sea.

Wintner and Margaret left Sir Vivian pondering over the complexities of a new military manoeuvre and made their way to the kitchen.

'You can call me Harry in 'ere if you like. I suppose you won't want to stay with us, I can't say I blame yer, although none of us are as bad as we look. It's just that we are a bit different from most.'

Margaret considered her position as Wintner plugged in the electric kettle. She had to stay somewhere. The £10 would not last for long and people that were 'a bit different' had so far given her more joy than the others.

'Harry, I wonder, could you give me a few more details as to what board I must pay, or what duties I have to do if I stay here. I am not qualified to do anything, but type and I'm not prepared to do that.'

Harry sat down with surprise and relief, he spoke quickly.

'Oh, yer don't need any qualifications and there's no need for you to pay board. In fact, we pay you. £3.50 a week as companion to Lady Hilda, that is on Monday, Tuesday and Thursday evenings and all day Sunday. Ahem, 'er Ladyship 'as a problem, you probably gathered, you would have to be discreet. . . .'

Margaret had noted the requests for sherry and brandy. Already her protective impulses had begun to change the alcohol to tomato juice.

'Everybody I've ever met has had some problem or another, I don't understand other people's problems, but I can accept them. I'll stay here for a time if you like, but I shall be working during the day. Your terms are very reasonable and if you think I seem suitable, I'm glad to accept your offer.'

Steam from the kettle began to cloud the room and Harry quickly assembled a tea-tray.

'I can see there's more to you than meets the eye. Did you want to take up your tea to Lady Hilda's room?'

Margaret took the tray.

'It's the second on the left at the top of the stairs.'

He opened the kitchen door for her.

'How old did you say you was, love?'

'I didn't say', said Margaret. As she climbed the stairs she felt pleased with herself, she paused on the landing. Sometimes she felt fourteen and sometimes she felt forty. 'I suppose I'm

71

mature now', she muttered as she tapped Lady Hilda's door with her foot.

The single bed in the corner of the room caught Margaret's attention. She had only seen patchwork quilts in picture books. Here was the real thing. Lady Hilda recognised the appreciation.

'I'm glad you like that. Sit down, my dear. Here, put the tray on the table.'

She pointed to an elaborately carved round table, the legs of which were supported by four elephants who looked into the four corners of the room. There was a lot of space, the ceiling was high and the furniture sparse, apart from the table and bed, there were two shapeless armchairs, and a small nursing chair. Four or five enormous cushions were plonked like islands on a huge faded Indian carpet which covered the floor, one of the recesses near the fire-place contained shelves whilst a varnished ugly wooden box that appeared to have been converted into some kind of chair, took up the other. The walls must have been a creamy colour at one stage, but seemed to have adapted themselves to the nuances of light and time, now were part of, rather than a background to, the Indian paintings and tapestries which hung on them. Margaret sighed.

'I do like this room.'

It seemed an odd thing to say. The words had come out right, she had not been conscious of making any assessment.

'Good, do you like playing cards?' Lady Hilda peered under the table as she spoke.

'Oh yes, I love cards', said Margaret.

Lady Hilda rose and bent down to look behind Margaret's chair. Margaret took this as an indication to leave and stood only to be confronted with Lady Hilda's face at rather close quarters. This gave her a mild shock as on closer scrutiny, the face looked as though someone had given it a sharp slap. The red gash that represented her mouth was no longer horizontal and had now transformed itself into a round blob.

The cheeks had disappeared, but nature had not been totally unkind. The light blue eyes still held a trace of past beauty. It was the eyes that seemed to speak.

'I'm sorry, dear, I've mislaid my teeth. They've always been problematic – it's as though they're not a part of me, so to speak.'

Margaret spotted the teeth which gaped from a half-full tumbler of whisky on the window ledge. The glass was drained and Lady Hilda savoured her teeth before she finally snapped them into place. She clicked as she spoke once more.

'You like sewing?'

'Yes, I used to do a lot of it with my Auntie, we made all kinds of things.'

There were no questions as to where Margaret was from, or what she did or what she hoped to do, there was no discussion as to duties or time. This was not entirely due to vagueness, Lady Hilda had a great respect for privacy. The teeth might have upset some of the former tweeded, sensible shoed legion of companions, but this one had not seemed disconcerted at all.

'You must feel tired after your journey. Your room is the one opposite this one. There's a water buffalo head just over the door, you can't miss it. Remove the head if you like. Vivian never comes upstairs so it won't be missed. Come I'll show you.'

Margaret took Lady Hilda's arm. It was a gesture of necessity as much as an offer of pending friendship. Wobbly progress was made to Margaret's quarters.

Apart from an Indian carpet and brown velour curtains drawn across the bay window, the room was bare. There was no time for questions.

'Furnish it yourself, take what you like from the two store rooms at the end of the corridor. Wintner will carry the heavy stuff for you. Make the room your own, rearrange it as often as you like. In India I was always rearranging, I seemed to have stopped now, but I dare say you will want to and that's good. I'll leave you now.'

Lady Hilda nodded and tottered back to her room. An hour later, Margaret was ready for her bed with its Afghan fur coverlet. Three large cushions formed a transportable sofa against one wall, there were two low round black tables, a small wardrobe containing her clothes and a tiger skin pinned to the wall. She sat on the cushions sipping her cocoa. I like it better than Runnock, but how do I make it my own? I suppose that's why it's necessary to rearrange. It's not that things look different, but you see different as you go along. Already the tiger skin was being mentally expelled along with Cora, Len and Mr Barraclough. The contemplation was shattered by a loud crash which came from the room opposite. Margaret opened her door quietly to hear heavy breathing followed by a long groan.

'Oh, my God, oh my God.'

The words came from Lady Hilda's door.

She was dragging herself along the floor by her elbows looking like some valiant polio victim. Her route had taken her from her bed to the centre of the room where she was resting her arms on the low elephant table.

'Can I help at all?' Margaret spoke quietly.

She knelt behind Lady Hilda and placed her arm around her shoulder.

The light blue eyes gradually focused in Margaret's direction and the camera spoke.

'The throne, help me to the throne.'

Margaret took this as a reference to some past grandeur.

'I will, my Lady.' She then tried to turn Lady Hilda back in the direction of her bed.

'For God's sake, help me to the throne.'

Lady Hilda's tone sounded desperate, not imperious. She managed to point to the wooden box chair near the chimney recess before falling flat on her face. Margaret joined her in a kneeling position, together they crawled towards the chair. Lady Hilda lifted its seat and indicated its function. The commode relaxed Lady Hilda. She talked over the urgent spurts and trickling water sounds.

'I'm sorry, I'm sorry, my dear, you must be revolted.'

'No.' Margaret paused and pulled Lady Hilda's nightgown over the bare knees. 'No', she added, 'I'm not revolted at all.'

'Thank you, dear, I'll be all right now, you've been most kind, most understanding.'

Margaret left quietly, glancing back as she opened the door. If someone had told her yesterday that it was possible to maintain some dignity whilst sitting drunk on a commode, she would not have believed them. There was something which touched her on viewing the crumpled heap of womanhood urinating in the corner. The feeling in many ways was similar to what she had felt on her earlier fishing expeditions with Richard. She closed the door.

'I want to be truthful, I want to be innocent.' These thoughts passed through her mind as she drifted into fitful sleep. Her sub-conscious grouped people and events with no respect for sequence or place, slumber was more bewildering than being awake. In either state, the jig-saw puzzle did not seem to fit. It was necessary to be satisfied with fragments of pictures and flashes of people that were incomplete and ever-changing. If only the tapestry could keep still, she might be able to fit herself in somewhere.

'Are you awake, miss? Good morning. I've brought your tea. I'll put your cup on the table and we can move it next to the bed. There.'

Wintner moved quickly without sound.

'Thank you, Harry. I've never had tea in bed before.'

Margaret propped herself up. Wintner watched her for a while as she sipped the tea.

'It's better if you talked to me as it was first. I mean, it's easier for me.'

He looked down at the floor.

'Pardon?' She placed her cup on the table.

'I prefer being Wintner, I've got used to it, there's less trouble being Wintner.'

Margaret was puzzled.

'But you're the same person whether I call you Harry or Wintner aren't you?'

Wintner took up the tray and stood erect.

'No, miss, I'm not.'

The reply was definite.

'Oh, well, er – thank you, Wintner, that will be all.'

He nodded and left. 'Perhaps that's the answer', thought Margaret as she slid into her stockings. 'Play a role, take on a part.' She had not considered that, in her case, there might be some difficulties in casting.

There were two doors that led to the entrance of 24 Dean Street, London, W.1. The doors were adjacent to one another. The larger door led into a newsagent's whose customers all appeared to be men. Most of them left the shop with a *Standard* or a *News* wrapped around some other kind of magazine or newspaper. The other door remained open to reveal nothing but a peeling cream-painted wooden staircase which rose steeply as a switchback. It climbed and curved into floors and half landings just as dangerously. The stairway led to varied forms of paradise which were indicated by four names painted on the wall of the hall-way:

First floor: Sagittarian Films Inc.
Second floor: Changing Scene Recording
Third floor: Awkward Agency
and the fourth floor: Anita Colonic Irrigation Health Specialist.

It was Hilda's idea that she should visit the agency. Margaret had almost forgotten about it in the six months that had elapsed since she first arrived in London. She had absorbed the city slowly making short excursions with Hilda and occasional trips to the night life with Adrian. For much of the time, he bored her as his conversation for the most part seemed to have regressed to either adulation or denigration of the latest pop-star or cult film-star. His friends were full of gossip or injury and treated her like a walking, talking doll. There was plenty of attention, but no interest. She felt like a bit of decoration whilst she was with them. The potter was different.

She would watch him at the wheel under the post office in the late afternoon. As the day rose and took shape in his hands, he introduced her to Vivaldi, Joan Baez, Scott Fitzgerald and Thomas Mann. He gave her beautiful picture post cards from galleries all over the world. He talked about Kafka, Hermann Hesse and Christ. He was always sad and Margaret helped him to smile from time to time. She told him about Richard and he'd said, 'Keep that, keep that with you' and had cried into his clay.

Adrian had declared him a social disaster after the third meeting and 'dropped' him. Margaret called him her pottery teacher but she never touched a piece of clay. There was no curriculum to her afternoon classes, but the course proved to be wide and full of interest and influence. Margaret felt she had lost more on the day that she found the pottery empty (save for the sandals and clay) than she did when Adrian left for a tour of Australia in a Whitehall farce. Adrian gave her two Shirley Bassey records as a parting gift. She mislaid the records later, but never parted with the sandals.

Her thoughts had carried her past the third floor and she was greeted on her descent by a portly well-dressed man in a bowler hat. He raised his hat.

'Miss Anita?' he enquired hopefully.

'Just a few more steps up', Margaret answered politely as they crossed on the stairs. Clouds of cigarette smoke drifted from the half-open door of the 'Awkward Agency'.

'You'll probably be too tall. From the description here it seems they want a midget or a dwarf. Give it a try anyway, if you wear your sneakers you'll drop four inches.'

The woman's voice presented the information and suggestion in the same manner as someone selling a car or a country cottage that did not quite fit the needs of the client in hand.

'Christ, I'm only four foot five, that ought to be good enough. What would the fire brigade want with a midget?'

'It's not the fire brigade, it's an insurance company. Specialised in fire. It's a pity there's nothing wrong with your glands, Clive. You're just naturally small. Somehow, I don't think that's quite what they want, but as I say, give it a try.'

The telephone rang, the small man left the office not noticing Margaret and clumped down the stairs in shoes with heels so high that they must have placed him beyond accident risk protection.

Margaret entered the office without knocking and sat quietly on a chair just inside the door. The woman on the telephone noted her entrance without any change of facial expression – the eyes never moved. She could even have been blind. She spoke into the telephone and looked fixedly in front of her.

'Yes, I have just what you want, what time is the audition? He'll be round tomorrow – wrestles in his spare time. No he's never done after shave, only beer and boots. Nothing camp. He'll be fine – see him first and we can discuss the percentage later. I'll contact him now, 'bye.'

She spoke to a sweet looking elderly lady who looked like everybody's mother (she did, in fact, specialise in such roles when they came up, but had been over-exposed in the last year).

'Mavis, trace Lenny Manning for me, you'll probably find him at the "Bona Fide Club" or at his mother's place in Wapping – tell him this one could be big, p'raps a TV commercial.'

Mavis took up the green telephone which was the only semblance of industry on her desk.

'OK, E.B.-J. The temp sent a note to say she couldn't get in today, she might be in Wednesday or Friday.'

Mavis spoke as she dialled.

'Bloody typists. Yes? Yes?' Margaret realised the second time round that she was required to speak.

'I've come about a job, you were recommended to me by a mutual friend.'

'How fast do you type and what time do you get up in the morning?'

Estelle Bingham-Jones raised both hands and pushed the large false bun even further on to the top of her head, stabbing it with fresh pins as she did so. These were transferred from her mouth so that she spoke through clenched teeth.

'I came here with the hope of doing some modelling, I don't wish to type. I'm most adaptable and if you look you can see that I have a very expressive face.'

Margaret's cool audacity forced Estelle to spit the two remaining pins from her mouth on to the desk and Mavis swung her chair round in Margaret's direction.

'I can look like almost anybody if I have to, my face can change from day to day.'

Estelle put her head down on her desk like a tired magistrate brutally dismissing the case before her. Mavis ambled over to Margaret and took her gently but firmly by the arm.

'Try number thirty-four dear, there are jobs for young girls there.'

The motherly grip had tightened on Margaret's arm as she was propelled towards the open door.

Margaret was not surprised, she had expected a cold reception and planned her tactics accordingly. She outmanoeuvred Mavis on the landing in a brief square dance.

'I'm sorry, I've left my handbag under the chair.' She entered swiftly and reached for her bag. Only when she spoke did Estelle Bingham-Jones look up.

'Lena sent me here. Lena Menton.'

'What!' E.B.-J.'s nostrils twitched like a cat or a rat.

Margaret fixed her eyes on the bun which just touched a flowering Busy Lizzy perched on the window ledge behind the desk. The effect of Lena's name was lethal and Margaret savoured the power of the ammunition. Was the nose sniffing fear or excitement? Probably both. Mavis had entered and a gesture from E.B.-J. seated her. Margaret smiled like a benevolent conquistador who is sorry she is here, but has no choice, invasion being the pathway of duty.

'Photographs', snapped E.B.-J.

'I'm sorry, I have none and I can't tell you where she is, it's not that Lena is secretive, mysterious you might. . . .'

Margaret was cut short.

'That bitch, mysterious?'

E.B.-J. placed her hand to her wide brow and leaned on her elbow, she spoke in a voice which was much too subdued to be relaxed.

'I don't want pictures of Lena, darling, I want nothing of her. I can remember her well enough, but I am trying to avoid nightmares. The photographs, I mean', she paused, 'Do you have any of yourself? It's customary to send them to possible clients.'

E.B.-J. clearly cherished no affection for Lena, but held her in some respect or fear. On the strength of these qualities Margaret was being offered help by a woman who held no immediate appeal. It might be dishonest to accept it but, on reflection, she justified receiving it as part of her loyalty to Lena.

'I have some, mostly in fancy dress. Snapshots, but I'm afraid they were taken quite a long time ago.'

Margaret's confidence ebbed. E.B.-J. sat quietly, turning her dark brown eyes on to Margaret's throat.

'If I gave her a shawl and a fan, she'd be away, Olé.'

Margaret sniggered at the thought and quickly changed it into a smiling nervous apology.

'Aa, – ha-ha, ha-ha-ha- – I don't suppose snapshots would be much use, and you would want something more recent I suppose?'

'Recent and professional, I can find you a good photographer for £45. Of course, there is no guarantee that we can sell you even then, but the better the photographs the better the chance.'

Estelle stood up; much to Margaret's astonishment she was very tall. Perhaps it was the bun or the low ceiling, like the tower in Pisa, she leaned slightly.

'Well I haven't saved that much yet. . . .' Margaret had almost conceded a retreat when she was interrupted by a woman with a very short tight skirt who hobbled into the room and stood only a foot from E.B.-J.'s desk. The legs from behind were of the solid quality found underneath Victorian table tops; this was odd as they held up a small frame and a well-shaped head with an urchin cut hair style.

'If you gave me the chance I could sell myself. I always have done one way or another. What is so special about this client?'

Margaret kept her thoughts to herself. If she listened, a few tricks of the trade might pass her way.

'Am I too late? I never got your message until an hour ago. I've raced from Earls Court. The other girl in my flat forgot about it, she's a teacher too. You wouldn't think a teacher would be so selfish would you?'

Estelle ignored the question; personal details were only significant if they affected business.

'There's a job for you over at Shepherds Bush – photographs before and after job. It's a straight £30 deal. They're expecting you at five, expenses paid.'

Estelle wrote an address on the pad before her as she talked.

'Above or below? £30 seems scarce, back home I could have made twice that selling shoes. I miss the sun, it never stops bloody raining here.'

Margaret shifted the girl from Sydney, Australia, to Earls Court, to Dean Street in three quick moves. Check – if she were on the beach, she'd have to keep her legs covered.

'It's above', said Estelle.

'You'd better clean up a bit, dear, before you go', said Mavis soothingly.

'There's cream in the cupboard. Do you mind using this mirror? It's a case of having to make do, as you only have just under an hour to get there in time.'

The mirror was straightened and the pot of cream ready before the girl had time to get over to them. Her face was pleasant enough, but there were no outstanding features. The heavy make-up gave the complexion a peach-like quality, but there was nothing special about that. Any number of girls looked like peaches, you saw them on the Underground every day in spite of the weather. However, the particular peach in question revealed far more bruises and blemishes when peeled than Margaret could ever have imagined. The cream dissolved the skin in ten seconds to reveal a female 'Dorian Gray'.

'Not too bad.' The lady from 'down under' studied the pimples and mattered pustules with evident satisfaction. Her face was a volcanic terrain. She squeezed the minor eruptions gently.

'I'll just ginger them up a bit before I go – there. It's not "Wonder Smear", is it?' she asked.

Estelle shook her head.

'It's a new one.'

'See you then, mate', the girl said as she hurried out towards the prospect of a quick £30. Knees bent, face aflame, she clattered down the stairs well pleased. She had earned £200 from the acne in less than six months.

Mavis smiled and sighed.

'Dedicated girl, Philippa. Dedicated.'

E.B.-J. took a little cream from the pot and gently smothered her long white hands. She tended them carefully, stroking herself as though she were a costly fur or a Persian cat.

'You see, my dear, this job is not all glamour. Advertising and modelling is based on truth. If you have something truthful to offer as well as being different, it might sell – with careful handling, of course. In your case, there's no denying that you're pretty, and a pretty young face can do well in London. The field is wide and perhaps I could help you with some contacts if you keep in touch.'

She smiled brightly and lit a cigarette.

'Had you thought of being a hostess at any time?'

She puffed out a cloud of smoke. Margaret waited until the screen cleared before she answered. Her dismissal had been presented as a favour which she sought to reject.

'I've been called lots of things, but never pretty.'

She lapsed into her Runnock accent; somehow it helped the delivery. 'Then, I suppose you're the expert, so thanks. I know you won't mind me disagreeing with you on another point. I am different. Everybody I know has thought so, I change almost every day. You probably won't recognise me tomorrow.'

'Tomorrow, dear?' Mavis sounded a little concerned.

Estelle stubbed out her cigarette and leaned forward.

'I need some photographs and you need a typist, I'm very fast – seventy words per minute – what are your terms?'

There was a pause before E.B.-J. answered and once more she spoke very quietly.

'I give the temp £14 if she completes a full week.'

'That sounds fair', said Margaret as she stood to leave. 'Oh, would you mind working out my payment by the hour? From what you have said about my predecessor, she was very slow. I can probably cover all her work and more in half the time, and I'm sure you won't want me cluttering up the office for five days when I need only be here three. What time would you like me in the morning?'

84

'Nine', Estelle whispered.

'Nine then', said Margaret and left.

'The little slag – the cheek of her', said Mavis indignantly.

E.B.-J. lit another cigarette.

'She could earn us a lot of money.' She gave another hitch to her bun. 'A lot of money.'

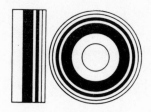

Of all the villages, Margaret liked the West End least of all. It was the centre of everything, but people visited it and left it. This constant feeling of transit took the glamour from the clubs and theatres. The place had the trappings of a holiday affair, fourteen days of excitement, perhaps love, all for £90. That was all there was to it though, just fourteen days. She hurried through the rush-hour crowds anxious to get back to Bayswater, her village; it held special comforts for her, it absorbed her. There were still parts of London unknown to Margaret, the names held delight. What went on in Tooting Bec and how did people travel in Stoke Newington? The man in front of her at the Underground ticket office booked to 'The Elephant'. She had heard people say that they not only lived at 'The Elephant', but down it, and in it. It was still a source of wonder that you went down in an escalator and popped up ten minutes later somewhere completely different, yet it was all

London. So far, she had never met anyone born in London; she had met people from Gateshead and Banbury, Kent and Melbourne, but never a Cockney. Wintner spoke like one at times, but when Margaret had enquired, he was rather hurt, and informed her in a most curt manner that he was from Ilford, Essex. Apart from the blocks of Council flats which rose like separate fortresses and compounds in all the villages, the whole city resembled a rehabilitation centre for displaced persons. Margaret had come to like it very much indeed. She smiled as she handed in her ticket to the West Indian guard at Bayswater. For one reason or another, she had always felt displaced and she was not black or Jewish or homosexual. There seemed to be no particular category for her minority.

Apart from formal courtesies there was little communication with Sir Vivian or Wintner. Meals were served, pleasantries exchanged and doors were shut in the bottom part of the house. 'Lady' had been dropped from Hilda who was now a friend. On arriving home Margaret found her just waking from a deep alcoholic sleep. Wintner brought in some tea and biscuits and Margaret helped Hilda handle the cup as she gurgled and yawned herself back to life. She had become thinner, her hands trembled a little now, her frailty made her smaller so that it was almost like holding an injured sparrow. She needed to be held, but instinctively disliked the physicality involved. Propped up like a puppet, she withdrew into the supporting cushions behind her. Margaret had attempted all manner of means to wean her from the drink. She had tried hiding it – this only increased the craving and resulted in tantrums. Long walks were attempted in the hope that sleep would follow exhaustion. It did, but only after a half-bottle of whisky had been drained beforehand. Pontoon worked better than anything else. The game was new to Hilda who exchanged it for bridge. There was more chance involved and Margaret had become much too adept a pupil at bridge, too sensitive to lose intentionally – the outcome of each hand had become boringly predictable. Besides, they could talk through pontoon. This talk placed Hilda's liver less at risk.

'I'll stick', said Hilda fanning herself with the three cards. 'You have no family at all then? Your Aunt Florence was not a blood relative?'

'I've bust', said Margaret. 'No, not a soul, my Mam is alive though so I've been told, but if she had wanted to see me she would have come, wouldn't she? People say blood is thicker than water. I would have loved to have been part of a real family.'

'Your deal. It's prone to disorders', said Hilda.

'What?'

'Blood. Blood can be leukaemic, toxic, or any number of things. I would have been better off without it. If I had been born like you and not bred, I think that I would have known great happiness.'

She pondered this. 'At least, for a time.'

Margaret said, 'I'll stick. You make yourself sound like a race-horse.'

'I was just that as a girl, a young girl. An attractive filly entered for Maiden Stakes at fixed odds, the outcome was a foregone conclusion. Vivian was at Eton – only a boy when our marriage was arranged.'

There was no bitterness in the tone, but its sad acceptance in the midst of the cards gave it an added desolation.

'You weren't a Muslim were you?'

Hilda laughed. 'No dear, it was all to do with blood.'

'Did you marry him without knowing him. I mean did you see him?'

'At intervals, yes, but one married in order to know in those days. I did know someone before him. That is, I knew someone in the biblical sense of the word.'

'Oh, Hilda, you mean a lover?'

Hilda nodded and lay back on the cushions transported by recollection and a captive audience.

'I was referred to by the rest of the family as the afterthought.

My Mother was almost forty-five when I was born, so there was no question of brothers or sisters for company. My two brothers and elder sister were already parents themselves by the time my christening came around. My appearance was most indiscreet. It's difficult to hide a baby, but my family had a very good try. I saw little of my mother or father until I was six or seven and then she took on my education – sewing and reading for two hours each day.

'A series of governesses filled in bits here and there until I was fifteen. Vivian and I were encouraged to play with one another three or four times each year. We were most considerate children, we never shared an activity, but always paralleled it. If he were tending a wounded soldier, I would care for an injured doll. You might say our sympathies were aligned, but not enjoined, and it's odd that's the way it always remained. Could you pour me a little sherry dear, or whisky, whichever is to hand. Thank you.'

Hilda sipped the whisky.

'Vivian was commissioned in India, and it was felt I should join him at seventeen, as his wife of course. My parents were not in the best of health, and I was more in the way than ever. I spent most of the time in the grounds and it was there that I met the gardener's son. He was my Ferdinand, your Richard. There was no coyness, no questioning. Our meetings were never arranged, I remember him once taking his boots off in the gazebo for fear of muddying my dress, this was silly as the floor was . . .' she had fallen asleep, only the snores filled in the gaps of the story.

Margaret placed the whisky glass away from its perilous position at the edge of the table before deftly removing Hilda's teeth and settling them comfortably for the night. Last week the gardener's son had been an Indian male servant (who spoke with his eyes), before that there was a young music tutor and before that a Sepoy sergeant. Real or imaginary, Margaret never found any of them dull. She drew the heavy curtains and collected the paraphernalia of tea-cup and whisky glasses on to the tray and made her way downstairs towards the kitchen. In all the fairy stories that she had ever read, they revealed that if a girl was orphaned, poor and good, it usually turned out that she was not poor at all. In fact, by some quirk of fate or passing magic, her true royal heritage had only been denied her for a time, her true status as a princess was usually returned just before or after she had met her prince. She balanced the cups more carefully on the tray. Perhaps I have blood in me somewhere in the past. This comforted her and she straightened her back as befitted her birth as she descended the stairs. I have all the qualifications, I am poor, I am an orphan. She paused on the half-landing and thought of the afternoon spent with E.B.-J. She shrugged her shoulders and rattled the tea-tray. If I'm not good, it's not altogether my own fault. The shrug and her doubts about her own goodness had disposed the grandeur from her by the time she reached the foot of the stairs. It was then that she heard the shouts.

'For God's sake see to yourself first.'

Sir Vivian's voice boomed urgently from his study. This was followed by a thud and a gasp.

'But, sir, you're hurt, your leg, it's. . . .'

Wintner's groans were curtailed by more orders.

'Never mind about my leg, man, get the iodine. It's in the knapsack – apply it to your shoulder, jump to it, man, that's an order. Ah-a-a-a-a, do it now. Ah-a-a-a.'

Sir Vivian's own pain seemed to have increased, there were more grunts of heroic despair and whispered agony and Margaret felt obliged to put her ear to the door.

'Tear the cloth away. How does it look, Wintner?'

'It's bad, sir, as bad as it can be. Shattered I'm afraid, completely shattered.'

'Knot the cloth above the knee-cap. Tighter, man, tighter, now turn it as hard as you can ah-a-a-ah. That's it – pour on the iodine.'

90

'Sir, you need a surgeon. I think it will have to . . .' Wintner hesitated.

'Well speak up, don't dither, where's your guts?'

'It will have to come off, sir. The bottom of your leg must come off.'

'There's no time for shilly-shallying now – use my sabre and turn the knot tighter.'

Wintner stammered, 'I can't, sir.'

'Can't, can't, what do you mean, you can't? Get on with it, man.'

'I can't do it, sir, I can't do it.' Wintner's voice broke into sobs.

The situation was serious enough to warrant a dispensation of the usual rules of privacy. Margaret pushed open the door with her foot – if there was an emergency she might be needed. She was more shocked than confounded by what she saw, so much so that the tray dropped from her hands and crashed to the floor. Wintner was sitting by the fire darning a grey woollen stocking whilst Sir Vivian sat at the table near the window engrossed in some kind of individual chess using soldiers instead of bishops, knights or pawns. Neither of them made any attempt to move. They chose not to view the broken crockery; the darning and the military chess just developed an intensity of concentration which went beyond the normal attention given to such pursuits. Margaret stood still, and gradually she lowered herself to the ground like a punctured balloon and began gathering the fragments of glass and china on to the tray, only her burning ears mirrored her shame and embarrassment. The two minutes spent clearing the floor seemed like hours; when the task was complete she stood to speak. No words came and she closed the door quietly. It was not in her nature to be predatory and she felt truly penitent. She hoped the game might be resumed but alas, there were no more sounds from the study that night.

The following morning she joined Wintner in the back garden. Half-a-dozen rose trees were being ruthlessly pruned.

In horticultural terms, it was a late exercise. Margaret took a rake and collected the shorn leaves and shoots into one pile.

'You 'ad better put some gloves on, miss, you'll tear your hands if you're not careful. Lovely flowers roses, but vicious to handle.'

He wiped the sap off the secateurs and placed them in the deep pocket of his blue overall. He pointed to the pile of briar.

'We can burn that lot at the top of the garden, miss, near the high wall. D'yer like bonfires, miss?'

He sounded like a child offering awkward conciliation for some past misdemeanour. This only increased Margaret's guilt which had transcended the previous night. She was moved by a wave of pity which added real conviction to her answer.

'I love bonfires, Wintner, you are such a thoughtful man.'

Together they listened to the snap and crackle of the twigs and as she watched the fiery sparks fly into the air, she felt part of some strange pagan rite that placed an indelible signature on trust and friendship. As the embers died, Wintner turned and nodded.

'All right, miss?'

'All right, Wintner', said Margaret contentedly.

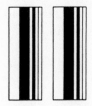

All that's said about Springtime and flowers
About children and fires w-a-r-m
Would be mine, Would be mine,
If things had happened differently.

In spite of Vivaldi, Margaret was still fond of current pop.
She sang as she prepared herself for the photographer. She
obeyed instructions carefully and encased her hair in the
sawn off foot of a silk stocking – this made her head smaller
than ever. Enmeshed in lisle, she looked like the white wife of a
Masai warrior; not wanting to project this image longer than
necessary, she pinned the dark brown wig carefully into place.
It was difficult to say whether the subsequent transformation
constituted any improvement, Margaret was not too happy
with the effect and Aunt Florrie would have thought she
looked common. Comfort came from Hilda who had ordered

a Pernod for breakfast instead of coffee because Margaret had so reminded her of the girl she had met in St-Germain.

Given a gesture, given a gesture,
He might be-e-e- just here with me.

The sorrowful yearning lyrics were belted cheerfully into the air. There was no question of association, there was no 'he' that she wanted to be with. Remembrance of her dead lover moved her only as a poem might, there was no ache. If he were with her now for example, what would she do with him? She stepped out boldly into the June sunshine. Already she could feel the warm rays on her bare arms and on the bare neck. The wig remained impervious to the heat, so that when Margaret reached the terraced house in Earls Court, her head felt as though it were inside a pressure cooker. She dabbed at the beads of perspiration which trickled down her forehead and brushed away the tiny sweat bubbles from her nose.

Larry Bonard heard the bell. He tightened his jeans by hitching them higher and buckling his heavy belt one hole further. Then he sat down to get his breath. The bell rang for the third time piercing the white walls of his home. The enormity of the room was exaggerated by the rush matting and sparcity of the furniture. Apart from the low double divan and two leather chairs suspended on single metal rods, it contained nothing. Pinewood shelves displayed a few books and a record player. The kitchen was concealed in a wardrobe, spot-lights, plugs and cameras took up one corner of the room. These dead instruments of imagination only served to heighten the room's clinical effect. Photographs studded the cork embossed wall nearest the bed – they looked ill at ease in this stark setting which was more like a dental surgery than a home. Another solitary penetrating ring spun Larry round in his chair, he sniggered and got up to greet his client.

'Hi there', he shouted.

Margaret had begun to walk away. She had gone some

yards down the street when she turned to see him standing on the top of the Victorian stone steps which led to the entrance of the house.

'Come on in, I've been waiting for you, sugar.'

If he had been waiting, he might have answered the door, thought Margaret, not wishing to place bad tempers or irritability before career. She let the clean cut, pale-jeaned man usher her in. She sank into a chair which moved disconcertingly. She was forced to sit bolt upright with one foot placed firmly on the floor. She had always hated feeling dizzy.

'Coffee?' Larry drawled as he produced a pot full from the wardrobe.

'No thank you', said Margaret and waited.

'Looks good, comes across just right, just fine.' He was referring to her spindle-heeled shoes, the black stockings with butterflies embroidered on them, the lime green skirt with a slit up the side, and the pink and white peasant blouse. He hadn't credited her with so much potential. If she appeared on the Bayswater Road after eleven o'clock at night looking like this, her arrest would have been inevitable. He grinned, showing small even teeth.

'Great, baby, just great.'

Margaret recrossed her legs, she felt a little self-conscious about the exposed butterflies which flew right from her ankle past her thigh. E.B.-J. had told her to be careful when she heard that Larry had offered to do Margaret's photographs for free. It was not in E.B.-J.'s nature to show cautionary concern for her employees. This made Margaret all the more determined to redefine the present situation before any work progressed. Margaret chose her words with extra care.

'Glad you like the clothes, I obeyed your instructions to the last detail. I'm hardly recognisable, am I?'

'Oh, I dunno, baby, the real you still comes through, you couldn't hide that altogether.'

Once again she chose not to argue, she got up from the chair and spiked her way over to look at the photographs. This was quite a task as her heels did not adapt well to the rush matting. ('What does he know of me? He's only seen me three times and then I was behind a typewriter.)'

The resentment gave her courage.

'You said there would be no SI involved, I don't want to waste our time.'

'SI?' he frowned very slightly.

Margaret coughed.

'Sexual Intercourse. I'm not interested in it, not on a work basis anyhow.'

He stood and grinned, showing the palms of his hands to clarify his good intent.

'Cookie, I give you my word.' He paused. 'Just a little play acting, some party games, that's all. I know you're a girl with imagination, I can feel the flow.'

He pointed to a picture of a nurse which was repeated on the photographic mosaic several times.

'She's my girl, that's Elaine, see.'

He touched one of the pictures with his hands.

'That girl is decent. Clean, you understand and I wouldn't do a thing to hurt her.'

Margaret felt a bit more reassured by this, although his regard for his girl friend's wholesomeness did seem a little intense.

'Is she from the States too?'

'Sure, she's a Boston girl.' Larry himself was from Bradford, Yorkshire, but since becoming a photographer, he had convinced himself and others that he was 'Stateside'.

'Yeah, when she has completed her training, we are going to marry, probably next Fall. We plan on having a house full of kids. That's what I want, a good mother who'll have decent kids. OK, let's shoot if you're ready. Perhaps you'd better stand over there, just do your number and I'll call the mood.'

He took a camera in his hands, Margaret positioned herself against the whiteness and the photographs were taken at five-second intervals.

96

'Over here, angry.' Click, he leapt and darted somewhere else.

'Here sad, really.' Click. 'Joyful, baby, joyful here.' Click. 'Content, honey – no content, that's better, you've just been given a lollipop, great.' Click. 'Now you're cool – bored, out of your head, baby, good.' Click. There was no doubting his professionalism. He was assured, confident and stricken with a strange anxiety whilst he was working. This left them both exhausted after the fifteen-minute session, so that they both flopped on to the ground when the films were all used.

'Oh, I enjoyed that', said Margaret. 'When will they be ready?'

'Huh?' he half asked.

'The photographs, today's pictures?'

'Oh, Thursday, I guess.'

His part of their contract was now complete and he chose not to pursue it further. He picked an imaginary particle of food from his teeth and then ran his tongue along them for any other particles of residue that might be clouding the glistening enamel.

'You ever thought of marrying yourself?' he asked.

'I've been asked, but no I haven't thought about it much, it's a big step, isn't it?'

'For the guy that wants to marry you, sugar, it would be suicide', he sniggered again. He'd done that a lot.

'If you're going to be rude, I'm not going to stay. You hardly know me, let alone say things like that.'

Margaret kept her voice down. She did not wish to sound shrill or out of control. He hauled himself into a chair and spun himself round wagging his finger in mock admonition as he did so.

'Naughty, naughty, sugar, it's my turn; we agreed on no fees in exchange for party games.'

Margaret didn't want to cheat him, but answered forlornly. 'I didn't think I'd just have to sit here and be insulted.'

'Wouldn't you say £40 worth of photographs was equal to

an hour of insults?'

Margaret sat on the other chair and lowered her head. If they started now, the torment would be over quicker. She was too frightened to race for the door. He stood over her.

'Oh, baby, you're not worth insults, trash like you ain't worth breath, let alone words. My God, if you could see yourself. Jesus Christ, what do you look like? You're a walking garbage bin, sugar, you know that? There's nothing of you on the outside and what is inside is rotting. Don't look at her, honey, don't look at my girl, I don't want that sweetness stared at by shit like you. No don't move, you just sit right where you are.'

He spun her chair round and round, she was forced to cling on to the seat with both hands to avoid being pitched to the floor. Her ingenuity did not suit Larry Bonard's purpose. He grabbed the back of the chair, stopping it with a jerk which jolted Margaret off the chair. She sprawled on to the floor putting her arms before her to break the impact of the fall. The floor covering scratched her arms and elbows and the shock it delivered absolved all determination that she might have had with regard to 'earning' the photographs. She rose unsteadily and placed her hand on the wall for support, she felt sick and retched two or three times as her stomach somersaulted.

'That's what happens to merry-go-round tramps, baby. There's no gettin' away from it, you're a tramp, you're not fit to. . . .' Margaret had had enough, she wasn't going to stay to listen to any more, she couldn't view the curled lips without horror and she had begun to cry, quietly inside. He had achieved his purpose, she had begun to suffer.

For some reason, Margaret stumbled towards the door next to the kitchen wardrobe instead of the door which led into the hall-way. It could have been the dizziness which had impaired her sense of direction. In any event, there was not much time to contemplate the darkness of the broom cupboard as a vicious shove in the small of her back sent her crashing into it. When the door banged behind her, she sank exhausted to the floor, her back pressed against the wall and her knees squeezed against her head. She closed her eyes hoping that when she re-opened them she might find herself in bed in Bayswater, only to find that the nightmare became more real. Larry began to work himself into a frenzy outside the door and his abuse had become more rapid and vile. As it gained in momentum it lost its impact, so that the words no longer caused her upset. The tirade became an incantation which, like most obscenity, was pointless. Margaret chose not to interrupt. Her physical discomfort occupied most of her thoughts, severe cramps were placing reef-knots in her back and leg muscles, the air had become foul in spite of the disinfectant smell from the mop near her feet and the heat caused her to perspire like a grilled chop.

It was hard to say whether she was asleep or half-cooked when she heard a knock on the door – not her door. The raving ceased. She listened.

'Is that you, Mr Bonard? It's Miss Haltenprice. The lady from the basement let me in. I've come about the fashion photographs for *Horse and Lady*.'

There was another knock.

'Hello, hello-o-o.' The coy voice was like a rainstorm in a desert. Margaret answered by rattling and banging the mop against the door. She heard Bonard open the door for the woman from *Horse and Lady* and timed her exit perfectly.

'Mr Bonard, I'm finished in here now, they're all developed.'

Margaret banged on the door again. 'Mr Bonard, they're all complete, your photographs are ready, could you open the door please?'

Margaret staggered out, one leg buckled under her, but she managed to remain upright. Bonard's recovery was remarkable, he smiled.

'Laura Haltenprice, editor of *Horse and Lady*, this is. . . .'

Margaret took advantage of his pause and introduced herself.

'Miss Trash, Trixie Trash, of the "Awkward Agency".' She proffered a sweaty palm. 'Pleased to meet you Miss Haltenprice, no delighted, I'm sure.'

Miss Haltenprice was rather taken aback, letting her hand slither past Margaret's outstretched one. She turned to Mr Bonard quizzically, silently asking for some explanation of the figure before her.

'We're doing something on disinfectant, a trade magazine job. It – er – kinda correlates housewives with bacteria. I mean – er – the idea is that a housewife who does not use disinfectant becomes a germ herself, eventually that is.'

Miss Haltenprice peered closely at Margaret.

'Good Lord, how original, what creativity. A human germ, I must say you do look the part, my dear. How incredibly versatile you models are becoming. I'm astonished.'

Margaret straightened her wig and added brightly, 'Oh, it's all in a day's work, Miss Haltenprice, though this particular job has required more concentration than others. I'll leave you to your work now, I can see you're a busy lady. Please don't bother to see me out, Mr Bonard. I'll take the film with me if you don't mind.'

Larry's composure cracked a little as he extricated the films from his camera and handed them to Margaret.

'What time is it?' asked Margaret sweetly. 'I always lose all sense of time when I'm working.'

'I'm early, nearly six I should say, dear', said Miss Haltenprice.

'Good heavens, I have over-stayed for almost an hour and a half, my agent will be furious. I'll take the cheque in with me to the office, Mr Bonard.'

'The cheque?' Bonard's voice had a strangled quality.

'Agreed overtime, it was in my contract, it should be round about £33, but as we are old friends, I'll make it a round £30.

Can you make it payable to "Awkward Agency", it's only fair to my agent Miss Bingham-Jones.'

Miss Haltenprice beamed approval, she respected professionalism. It was Larry's turn for performances. His face had gone quite pale and he seemed to find the process of extricating his cheque-book from his wallet problematic.

'Are you feeling all right, Mr Bonard?' asked Miss Haltenprice.

'Oh, yeah, fine, just great, only we had a tough session this afternoon.'

'Yes we did', added Margaret. 'Modelling is not all glamour, champagne and roses, as my agent Miss Bingham-Jones said to me only a few months ago. "Advertising and modelling is based on truth." If you have something truthful to offer as well as being different, it might sell.'

Miss Haltenprice was even more impressed.

'Quite right, my dear, quite right'.

Larry handed the cheque over. If he hadn't been mean by nature he might even have been admiring Margaret by now.

'Goodbye, Miss Haltenprice, I hope we'll meet again. I'm no horsewoman, but if duty calls one can but try.'

Miss Haltenprice stood as Margaret was shown to the door by Bonard.

'Bitch', he mouthed the words from the doorway absent from Miss Haltenprice's gaze.

'No, no, I'm not that, Mr Bonard.' Margaret leaned on the banister stretching both arms along either side. 'But that's what you wanted and that's what you got isn't it?' She crossed one foot carefully over the other. 'You see, I'm very good at my job. I was born to this, I'm not a novice, you did get what you wanted.'

He smiled ruefully.

'Yes, I guess so.'

She turned to leave.

'Say', he called after her. 'You're OK. You're OK.'

Most people were ignoring the small boy shinning along the branch which overhung the pavement from one of the parks in Redcliffe Square. It was a pity, for if they had stopped to look, they would have seen the kite which dangled appealingly from the twigs at the end of the branch. The kite hung upside down from its tailings which were loath to give up their honeymoon with the twigs and leaves. Margaret bent down to have a better look at the brightly smiling face which was painted on its frame. She considered doing a handstand against the iron railings to bring the picture in proper perspective, but her shoes were not up to it. She stepped out of them anxious to see whether the face was happy or sad. The branch descended nearer the pavement as the boy moved his weight along it. Margaret could now almost touch the tailings. She jumped and clutched the leaves and twigs of the branch and pulled it towards the ground, this enabled the boy to complete the rescue operation, the weight of the branch took up all her strength and concentration. She did not let go until the boy, kite in hand, stood behind her, they both watched the branch shoot up into place showering them with leaves and pollen as it did so. It was then that the policeman spoke.

'I could arrest you for that you know. I'll have your name and address anyhow. Haven't I seen you around here before?'

'My name's Margaret Davis, I'm staying with Sir Vivian and Lady Bland in Bayswater.'

'Yes, and my name's not Dixon of Dock Green. Clear off. This is a residential area, there's no business for you here.'

His face was nasty and the lips curled in much the same way as Larry Bonard's had done. The boy had not moved. Awed by the uniform, he did not speak up in Margaret's defence, but slowly he turned the kite round and held it high above his head for her scrutiny. It was smiling and one eye winked. The slight damage below the other eye gave it a tear. This was enough to help Margaret back into her shoes and get her back to Bayswater without dropping from fatigue.

E.B.-J. stood at the small window behind her desk and watched Mavis clean up the mess of spilled coffee. Rivulets of murky brown fluid were trickling over the sides of the desk whilst Mavis clumsily absorbed the central pool of coffee with a large wad of blotting paper. The mopping up over, Mavis looked towards E.B.-J. The younger woman shook her head, she didn't want another coffee. Another fierce pull at her cigarette showed Mavis that she could offer no kind of sympathy which might help her employer's present discomfiture. She spoke lamely, 'She might have got delayed in the Tube or overslept. It's probably something quite simple like that. It's only half-past ten.'

E.B.-J. opened the window and looked out into the street for any sign of Margaret and Mavis retreated to the kitchen injured more over E.B.-J.'s concern for the girl than she was by the harsh rejection of her condolence. E.B.-J. cared for the girl and Mavis felt her concern yielded a weakness in her character that she had not seen before. Perhaps it was time to look for another agency. E.B.-J.'s voice soliloquised rather than conversed.

'She's never late, never. Totally reliable, she would have telephoned if anything had happened at home to make her late. She's normally here before both of us. If that skunk Bonard has touched her, I'll make him burn for it. It's my fault, I shouldn't have let her go, she might be hurt, or need help. . . .' She could not hide the relief on her face when Margaret opened the door and walked into the office.

'I'm ever so sorry I'm late, there's something wrong with the Circle Line, you've never seen such crowds waiting for the buses. The Tube Station was closed.'

Margaret draped her coat behind her chair and uncovered her typewriter.

'You see', Mavis called from the kitchen. 'Perhaps we'll all have a cup of coffee now.'

She said this like an uncomprehending parent giving careful advice to an adolescent child. ('Mother knows best.')

The last retort caused E.B.-J. to snort in irritation.

'Any letters or claims for me?' asked Margaret.

'No, none that won't wait.'

E.B.-J. took her coffee from Mavis.

'I've some other work for you, a bit of modelling.'

Margaret spluttered over her drink as her employer talked more rapidly. Any form of kindness, either her own, or that of someone else, always embarrassed her.

'It's nothing much, just two hours of background work, it's a beginning. You'd best drink up quick as you're due at Lancaster Gate at quarter past eleven. Fill in the agency form before you go and don't forget to hand in your introduction docket, you won't need to audition.'

'But photographs, I haven't got . . .', Margaret stumbled on, surprised at her good fortune.

'They won't be needed. Drink up your coffee.'

Mavis looked on, scarcely revealing her contempt, rendered dumb by jealousy. Margaret recovered a little as she took her docket from E.B.-J.

'It's 15 per cent to me on your first job, and 10 per cent for any following.'

Mavis relaxed a little, this was more like the old firm once again.

'It's not my first job.' Margaret handed over Bonard's cheque to E.B.-J.

'I did some extra work for Larry Bonard yesterday afternoon. It's made payable to the firm. Fifteen per cent is yours then.'

E.B.-J. held the cheque by the tips of her fingers.

'It was legitimate, there was a witness, Miss Haltenprice, editor of *Horse and Lady*. I used my modelling name.'

'Your modelling name?' Mavis spoke from the back of her throat and E.B.-J.'s jaw lost its composure to the point of her open mouth becoming a question mark.

'Trixie Trash, it's Trixie Trash', said Margaret.

'Trixie!' exclaimed Mavis. 'Why that's what my old Aunt

called her cocker-spaniel bitch. Trixie Trash, what in God's name is this firm coming to? You can't land us with a label like that.'

'She can', said E.B.-J. flatly as she folded the cheque.

'I'll be off then', Margaret gulped her coffee.

'Take the day', called E.B.-J. before breaking into paroxysms of giggling followed by raucous laughter, which had lain untouched at the bottom of her stomach for years. It was minutes before she could contain herself and pay some attention to Mavis who was sitting in a sulky stupor at her desk. She took pity on her.

'Could you wash these summer gloves for me, they're a bit grubby, don't you think?'

Mavis turned on her maternal beam and felt wanted again, although the recurrent tittering and light-heartedness which filtered from E.B.-J.'s desk throughout the rest of the day made her feel as though she had lost a daughter.

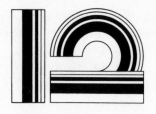

Margaret tidied Lady Hilda's room as though she were a constructive butterfly. She flitted silently around it, folding clothes, recovering drained whisky glasses which had been secretly placed behind cushions, dressers and curtains. The bowl of roses were well past being decorative or even sadly beguiling in their last moments. She decided to replace them. Lady Hilda slept soundly. Margaret looked towards her as she lifted the rose-bowl. One eye opened as the petals scattered themselves on to the carpet. The eye closed again and Margaret looked towards her as she picked up the petals from the floor and placed them carefully amidst their now shattered birthplace. She sat beside Lady Hilda and placed a glass of orange juice on the stand near her pillow.

Lady Hilda's face seemed to shrink with every week that passed. Her arms which lay over the coverlet did not require an X-ray as the translucent skin merely covered the veins and

bones beneath it like tissue paper. She was lamentably weak.
She had continued to drink a lot and ate little. Lady Hilda did
not wish to die from some malignant disease, nor did she want
to suffer and die from the post-operative effects of a surgeon's
knife. Like the roses – fading appealed to her more and she
was not unhappy with the direction that her alcoholic drift
was taking her. She breathed quietly in her slumber, indicating
to Margaret that she was wide awake as Lady Hilda's normal
sleeping habit was never void of snort and snore.

'Your orange juice is here, stop pretending. I know that you
are awake.'

Lady Hilda opened her eyes immediately and sat up in bed
as Margaret propped her up with pillows and cushions.

'What did you say was here, dear?' Lady Hilda asked
hopefully.

'Orange juice.'

'Oh, what a pleasant surprise', said Lady Hilda meaning
exactly the opposite. 'I'll drink it later.'

Margaret wanted to say that the roses would last longer if
Hilda could refrain from tipping her orange juice into the
rose-bowl the minute her back was turned, but it was no use
expecting her to feel any guilt about the plight of the flowers,
when her own condition offered no regrets for her.

'I didn't want you to feel harassed before you left. I must
say you look very pale this morning, dear. Are you nervous
about work? I shouldn't be if I were you. I wasted such a lot
of my life in nervousness, it's so dehydrating; and all because
of people whom one has absolutely no real interest in meeting.'

Hilda tightened the front of her hairnet as she spoke and
tucked the sparse curls back under it. She shook her head sadly
and added apologetically.

'Competition breeds snobbery.'

Margaret took a slip of paper from her pocket and passed it
on to Hilda.

'No, I'm not nervous. There is my brief; as you can see it
doesn't say much. "Drab young housewife – suburban belt,

re. Palmers Green or Merton." I shouldn't think I'll have to compete very hard, although there must be quite a lot of women around who fit that description.'

Hilda, irritated by what she had read, sucked in her gums and cast the paper on to the side of the bed. Her lips made a loud smacking noise.

'Drab, drab, how can they expect YOU to look drab. How very unfeeling of them to offer you such a part. I was quite happy for you to be a French tart, no personal reflection on you, my dear, of course, but there is probably a bit of tart in all of us'; she pointed to the paper. 'That is an insult.'

She pursed her lips, folded her arms and blew a toothless whistling sigh of exasperation. Margaret did not wish to leave her in this state of indignation, particularly as it was on someone else's behalf.

'I thought like that too, Hilda, yet think of what the cause of the drabness might be. Think of what it might conceal.'

Hilda looked at Margaret and her pale blue eyes glinted with life.

'Conceal?'

'There was a case in the papers only last week of a woman who had re-married after her first husband had been reported killed in the war. In fact, he had returned and found her twelve years afterwards now married to a shoe store manager in Ongar. Apparently she loved both of them and hid the first one in the gazebo and commuted between the two. The story was unfolded because of the row over the funeral arrangements.'

'Good Lord, she didn't murder. . . .?'

'Oh, no she died from nervous exhaustion or something like that; the two men quarrelled over the seating arrangements in church and that's how it all came out.'

'How very ungrateful of them, but then gratitude wouldn't enter it.'

Prompted by her own words, Hilda leaned forward and pointed to a small drawer in the bottom of the dresser.

'Open that, dear, pull the drawer out and pass it to me.'

She rummaged through the contents as though they were the cast-offs of a jumble sale. The broken strings of pearls, bangles and necklaces were scattered about the coverlet as her bony fingers clawed their way through the glittering entanglements. She held up a tiny gold chain which supported a small rose not more than two centimetres in width dotted with red stones.

'There.' She dropped it over Margaret's head. 'They could be rubies, they could be glass. They were given to me. I have concealed them, please take them. A bit of sparkle next to your skin will keep any of the drabness from penetrating it.'

'I'll keep it, always', said Margaret who was most moved by the gesture.

'Oh, no, don't say that, dear. If you feel the need then give it away just as I have done. Possessions would be of far more use if they changed hands more often, I mean as gifts, not barter. I am so pleased that I have no children to pass things on to. Keeping things within a family is disgusting.'

Margaret frowned, Hilda puzzled her. Sometimes she talked like a queen and at others she sounded like a communist.

Observing people made Margaret view all forms of political category with a certain amount of cynicism and caution.

'I'll get Wintner to change the flowers', Margaret took up the bowl and made her way to the door.

'The yellow roses, dear, only the pale yellow, they are my favourite, tell him not to mix them. Good luck for today', she paused and added as though it were the last thing in her mind.

'And would you mind pouring me a small whisky before you go?' Margaret was about to counter the last request, but Hilda was prepared.

'I'd like to celebrate your career, dear, and you wouldn't want me to do that on orange juice, would you?'

Margaret met the request and only sighed with regret after she had closed the bedroom door and fingered the necklace.

At this moment, Margaret was sighing for different reasons as she sat on a trestle with four other rather plain-looking women waiting to be called before the camera. A middle-aged man in tight jeans and a white tee-shirt had previously given them tuition on 'the product' for half an hour. Their teacher must at some time in his life been subject to Stanislavsky training. He had urged them to think, feel and be their parts. His final words hung over them like an undecided rain-cloud. It was hard to concentrate on something which looked as though it would never happen.

'You desire to be a housewife', he had said. 'You are defeated, utterly defeated by floor cleaning. In fact, your posture, facial expression, indeed your whole being should reflect the discarded apathy of an abandoned floor cloth. Think on that, work into it, live and breathe as though you are just that.'

His urgent direction was followed by a screening from the costume and make-up department. The other three girls needed little help here, but Margaret's hair was covered with a plastic cap and her body disappeared under the folds of a shapeless grubby ochre smock. For some reason, the two ladies who scrutinised her had said that her face didn't matter.

The product was a floor cloth stuck on the end of a stick. It was possible to squeeze the water out of the sponge by sliding a lever up and down the wooden pole that it was attached to. It did save kneeling and wringing, but Margaret had tactlessly said she liked doing both these marriage-ruining occupations. A stern-faced representative presented her with a free gift of the product itself, whereupon she had caused a little disruption by holding it rifle-fashion and parading round the camera area. The other girls had not liked this too much, but the technicians and cameramen had to be called back to work from a spontaneous but noisy game of cowboys and Indians. She had regretted the game immediately afterwards; even as a young girl her 'showing off' as it was then termed had not always given her retrospective peace of mind. Sitting on the trestle she began to feel thoroughly disillusioned with herself – disconsolate and dejected. The tutor came over to her and told her that she looked just right – she brightened a little at this. After all, there was some progress from a human germ to a floor cloth and nobody could say that either of the two roles had lacked challenge.

The other girls continued sitting patiently on the trestle as though they were refugees on an abandoned railway station. Indeed, Margaret suspected that her imagination had run riot when the trestle began to rock rhythmically with the kind of insistence that a railway carriage offers. The fat girl on the end was responsible. Her eyes had become glazed and unseeing, her hands gripped the trestle bench with so much force that the knuckles sprouted from her fists like small white onions. Margaret began to wonder if it was necessary to put so much effort into being the part as the rocking increased. Her consternation increased when she perceived that one of the fat girl's eyes stared in a different direction to the other and a tiny spittle of saliva began to dribble from the left-hand corner of the girl's mouth.

None of the other girls were injured when the trestle toppled backwards. They picked themselves up with the unflurried exactitude of marionettes. The fat girl shook and squirmed on the floor, her face contorted by convulsions.

Mucus and saliva blurred even further the indistinguished contours of her swollen face. The technicians and cameramen formed a semi-circle and looked on.

'She's having a fit', one of them declared blandly.

This piece of information spread quickly so that the fat girl became the central point of interest. The crowd watched fascinated by the spectacle, compassion did not enter the situation.

'Somebody should push a pencil between her teeth in case she swallows her tongue', another voice urged action reminiscent of the arena at Rome.

A lady with a cardboard sticker pinned to her blouse

announcing her as 'Miss V. Jenks, Personnel' said, 'This is appalling, we ought to have been warned, they should have let us know. We will be behind schedule and with one girl less all the measurements for the camera angles will have to be re-taken. It's most inconsiderate.'

No one else attempted a move towards the fat girl, so Margaret folded her jacket and calmly placed it beneath the girl's head.

'I haven't wet myself, have I?' the girl whispered to Margaret who was kneeling beside her.

'No', said Margaret wiping away the last trace of the spittle from the girl's jaw.

'It's me pills, I should have had one at twelve, but they're in my coat pocket and I didn't want to upset things by moving around, I thought they'd call us sooner. If I take my pills this only happens in the morning. Early when I'm asleep.'

The main attraction of the show now over, most of the crowd of onlookers had dispersed. Only Margaret and the other female floor cloths remained to listen to the poor girl's apolo-getic explanation. Miss V. Jenks came over when all five were once more re-seated on the trestle.

'Sorry about your mishap, Pauline dear', she smiled a bright personnel smile as she spoke. 'There's no need to worry about it any more. We will pay you for the morning. You just go home and rest.'

'But I'm all right now', said the girl. 'It's over, it won't come again. Really it's just that I forgot my pill.'

Miss Jenks took her by the arm and began to lead her to the coat pegs.

'I quite understand, dear. As I said we will pay you for the morning, now you. . . .'

Margaret was shocked by the barbarism behind this sweet professional dismissal. She stood and waved the other three girls on to their feet with one imperious sweep of her arm.

'Wait a minute, Miss Jenks', she called.

The camera crew and technicians turned for the second act.

'It's nearly four o'clock, we have been here since eleven without a break, not even a cup of tea. Not that we wish to complain, we realise that we have to look fatigued and we are just that. As artists we accept such conditions.'

The other girls nodded agreement and Miss Jenks' fixed smile disappeared.

'But you must realise we are a team, our exhaustion has to be collective. Our Director will vouch for this. I'm afraid if Pauline leaves, we all do.'

The other girls nodded agreement and Miss Jenks left for the work-room whilst someone quickly delivered tea to the newly formed repertory company who refused to be divided.

'The crew think you're THE one here', said the tall technician with the grave face as he handed Margaret a cup of tea. 'You ought to be at the centre of the action, not "soft".'

'Soft?'

'Soft, yes background, the girl who is centre is still being rehearsed, that's why you are waiting around. She's as dim as a Toc-H lamp, can't tell her arse from her elbow and keeps grimacing at the camera.'

'I mustn't complain', said Margaret. 'This is my first job, is it obvious?'

'Yes, it is.' His honesty disarmed Margaret who looked into his eyes and wished instantly that she were not a floor cloth. She touched her plastic cap self-consciously, but could think of nothing to say and he became awkward. They were rescued by circumstance for at that moment the girls were called for use.

Chalk crosses marked their positions, their cleaning postures were all worked out to the last detail, creativity had to be internal. The only part of Margaret's anatomy on film was her bottom and the sides of her plastic cap. The Director said that her face might detract interest from the centre-piece who grinned mindlessly whilst she cleaned without effort. From what Margaret could see of herself in her first bit of work, she looked for all the world like an electric light bulb that had been switched off. It was hardly satisfying. However, before she left, no less than three people had asked for her telephone number, the Director, the tutor and the technician with the grave face. She felt generous and acquiesced to all their requests, not knowing whether they might lead to more work or more leisure pursuits of one kind or another, perhaps both.

'I've learned so much working with you, Trixie', said Pauline as she saw Margaret on to the 88 bus. 'You're a star, a bloody star. See you then.'

With these words sounding in her head, Margaret did not mind having to stand. What with one thing and another, she could hardly feel that her feet were on the ground any way.

'Pour yourself a cup of tea, miss, I am afraid I have some sad news, very upsetting news.'

Wintner's behaviour was most unusual, he had made no enquiries as to the events of Margaret's day as he normally did, there had been no observations with regard to the climate and no reference to his employers. He had waited for her coat as soon as she opened the door, in fact, she had glimpsed him standing at the gate only to disappear immediately she had come into view. He had requested her to come into the kitchen and remained standing even though she had seated herself.

Wintner's long-term service in HM Forces at home and abroad had given him a clear concept on acting on what was right and what was wrong. In the last analysis, this meant that what he decided to do was right. The events of the afternoon had forced him to make a decision, of its correctness there was no question. Sir Vivian had agreed. Yet both men were now nursing the injury of duty in their separate ways. Sir Vivian sat silent and morose in his study whilst Wintner stood awkwardly before Margaret. Finally, he flicked an imaginary speck of dust off the table and sat. Margaret, aware of his discomfort, spoke first.

'Do you think we could open the curtains a little, Wintner, it seems a pity to waste the daylight, we're not overlooked here.'

Wintner coughed.

'I'm afraid not, miss, they must remain drawn in the circumstances.'

'Circumstances?'

'Take a sip of your tea, miss, I am afraid that I have some sad news, very upsetting news.'

It was going to be more difficult than he had imagined.

'Oh, tell it me quickly then, if it's bad, tell it all at once.' She placed her cup down and her head leaned slightly to one side. She always did this when she listened.

'Ahem, Lady Hilda fractured her pelvis and broke her neck at approximately twenty past eleven this morning.'

There seemed no point in delaying the rest of the report. The expected shock of the information was less than expected, the slow tears that he witnessed signified a sad acceptance of the inevitable. 'From what we can gather, she was dead on arrival at the hospital. Perhaps this was as well, miss. As you know, her Ladyship had little time for doctors, if she had regained consciousness, she would have certainly resisted treatment. I believe as a very young woman, she flirted with Christian Science and she was involved in something similar during the period of time that she spent in the East. I had taken up some of the pale yellow roses that she was so fond of, the ones called "Afterword" – she insisted on arranging them herself. A few minutes later I heard her calling. She stood at the top of the stairs clutching a few of the flowers shouting, "Greenfly, Wintner, greenfly, greenfly." Then she toppled forward and fell slowly, if that is possible. I reached her before she had rolled to the foot of the stairs. There were no sounds coming from her, no blood either, only from the palms of her hands. I suppose the rose thorns done that, miss. Sir Vivian says there's nothing more to be done except grieve and he's begun already.'

The sad commentary was terminated by Margaret. It was the rose thorns that made her succumb to shock as Pauline had done to epilepsy. The teapot wandered from her hand and crashed to the floor spilling most of its contents on to her left foot. Her cry of anguish ended Wintner's hopes of gently explaining the impropriety of Margaret staying on in the house alone with two older men. Margaret sank back into the chair and moaned.

'Oh, oh, Hilda, my foot, Hilda, Hilda, my foot, my foot.'

Wintner decided to relieve the pain of the living first and concentrated on the foot. It was easier than the other because it was practical and did not require words.

'Put your foot in this, miss.' Wintner placed a bowl of cold water in front of Margaret who had failed to faint.

In spite of the pain from her foot and the awful account of Lady Hilda's death, she still remained physically, intellectually and emotionally intact. She groaned; it was a bit unfair of nature not to release her just for a few minutes from the dual torment that engulfed her. She plunged her foot into the water; the relief weakened her and Wintner seemed to be an echo.

'There, miss, put your foot on the towel, and I'll sprinkle some bicarbonate on it for you. I don't think that it will blister but it might be best if you rested it tomorrow.'

'You'd better let E.B.-J. know', Margaret murmured. She had begun to enjoy being comforted and nursed. 'The telephone number is in the little green book, it's in my bag somewhere. How did Hilda do it? I mean, was she. . . .?'

'Oh, no, miss, she tripped on her gown. It was unfortunate that she was standing at the top of the stairs at the time.'

Margaret began to blink and Wintner did not want to stay for the tears. 'I'll make your telephone call, miss.'

In his absence Margaret closed her eyes and offered up Anglo-Catholic, Primitive Methodist and Bethany Baptist prayers for her deceased friend.

'Oh my God', she whispered, 'Oh my God, because thou art so good.' She winced a little at this point.

If He were so good then why should this have happened? It was wrong to question His authority (Sister Bessie had told her this in the Baptist Sunday School). For Hilda's sake, it wouldn't be advisable to question Him right now.

'Oh my God, because thou art so good, give her an occasional glass of whisky, not too much, and – and grant her a Sepoy in Heaven. For the love of thy only Son our Saviour Jesus Christ. Amen.'

'Sorry to wake you, miss, but your friend, Miss E.B.-J., she insisted on coming round here, half-an-hour she said she'd take.'

'I was praying, Wintner.'

'Oh!' Wintner coughed again. 'Then I'll leave you to it for a minute or two.'

Margaret could not ignore the dripping tap. She found it worrying that something so trivial could distract her from thinking of her dead friend, her thoughts ought to have transcended such fripperies. She hopped over to the tap and twisted it viciously before returning to sink back into the chair. This exercise complete, she closed her eyes in the hope that more prayers might enter her head. The voices in the hall-way broke her reverie some fifteen minutes later. She was surprised to find that her thoughts had thwarted her votive intentions. For the most part, these had dwelt not on the deceased, nor on the Director who might have helped further her career, but on the grave-faced technician. She was wondering what he might look like if he smiled. Teeth were so important. . . .

'Pull yourself together, Harry, this is no time for a scene, we are all much older now. No don't. . . .' E.B.-J.'s voice spoke without its usual authority.

'It wasn't for want of searching. There wasn't a house in Wandsworth I didn't ask after you. I looked for years. From Putney to Balham. Stella, I can't believe it's you. I feel as though I'm going to fall apart.' Wintner half sighed, half spoke.

'Well don't fall apart now, if you do we might not be able to fit the pieces together again', said E.B.-J. 'Where's Margaret?'

'This way; still the same old Stella', said Wintner warmly.

Margaret received them both in a feigned state of semi-swoon. E.B.-J. was not fooled and spoke as though the day had passed without any untoward occurrence.

'They telephoned from the studio. They were pleased with your work, they have something lined up for you next week. A central job this time. I came round to see if you would be well enough. Two nasty shocks in the space of an hour, it could be too much for you.'

Margaret made a remarkable recovery, opening her eyes and gingerly placing the injured foot to the ground. The white crocheted stole had slid off one of E.B.-J.'s shoulders so that its fringes touched the floor as she spoke. Wintner retrieved it and placed it back on her shoulders. Then he stood behind her performing as an attendant would at the Court of Titania. The two of them had achieved a strange unison. What thaumaturgy had performed this was beyond Margaret's perception. She spoke, but her words did not break into their aura.

'It's kind of you to take so much interest in me. I'm sure I'll be on my feet again by next week. I'm sorry you have had to give up so much time. If I could have three days off work. . . .'

'Of course, of course, my dear', said E.B.-J.

'You will want to attend the funeral, miss – ahem!' Wintner coughed. 'And there is the question of accommodation.'

'What question?' E.B.-J. spoke for Margaret whose security had momentarily been wounded to the point where one is struck dumb.

'Ahem! Ahem! The situation here would be – er – delicate. The idea of a young woman in a house with two grown men; Sir Vivian has his reputation to consider. The whole business is giving us grave disquiet as we are both very fond of Miss Davis.'

'I quite understand', said E.B.-J.

Margaret wondered whether she were understanding Sir Vivian's reputation or the two men liking her.

'It can be overcome simply without difficulty or trauma. If I move here for a few weeks, no one will comment on a woman of my maturity staying here. Sir Vivian will need a little extra help in house-keeping during this sad post-bereavement period. I'm tired of travelling to Beckenham every night, so the move will compensate everyone.'

Margaret's speech went further down her windpipe at this suggestion and her eyes widened as she witnessed the rapture spreading across Wintner's face. It seemed to enter his sober clothing. He beamed and glittered as E.B.-J. continued.

'Providing all parties agree?' she turned to look up at Wintner who hovered behind her.

'Oh, they will, miss, all parties will agree. You might as well stay tonight. I can get the room overlooking the garden ready for you – the French windows look out on to the lawn. It's all nicely private. I can help you collect some of your things tomorrow. Perhaps you would like to see it now?'

'Why not?' said E.B.-J. 'Excuse us, my dear.'

The two passed into the corridor.

'Oh, Stella', whispered Wintner.

'Shush', said E.B.-J.

Margaret's foot was almost better, but E.B.-J. had insisted on her spending the rest of the week at home. Wintner had left the house to do some shopping (his excursions from the house were more frequent since Lady Hilda's death). Before leaving he had given Margaret some lunch and then expressed the opinion that Sir Vivian would die within three months. Sir Vivian sat on the garden seat where Wintner had placed him to get some air. According to Wintner, he had not eaten, spoken or slept since his bereavement. Margaret pulled her cardigan round her shoulders as she looked out on to the garden. The late summer afternoon had turned cold.

Sir Vivian looked beyond temperature change, the heavy breeze swirled the unpruned thorny boughs of the rambler rose dangerously near his unseeing eyes. Rose petals fluttered about him, some settling on his head, a pigeon had left its signature splattered across his shirt as if he were a statue. The only apparent sign of life was his runny nose.

'Oh to God, he had died in action', thought Margaret.

It wasn't good for someone of his bearing to go like this.

She opened the window and called out.

'Like a cup of tea?'

The feeble gesture failed to move the old soldier. The more Margaret thought about him the more committed she became. There he sat, mortally wounded and all she could think to offer him was a cup of tea. Florence Nightingale and Edith Cavell left the Crimea and Brussels and inspired Margaret to take new stock of her own natural resources. A pair of low black shoes, some black tights, Wintner's blue and white striped apron and a clean white kitchen towel tied firmly on to her head conscripted her for active nursing service within ten minutes. A strategically placed splodge of tomato ketchup gave her uniform an added touch of authenticity that would have made Eisenstein proud. Certainly, it gave Margaret the extra verve and éclat which so often separated her performances from the norm.

She ran into the garden clutching a great armful of old dust sheets that had accumulated in spare rooms throughout the house. She dumped them a few yards in front of Sir Vivian's feet, added a little paraffin and set the murky bundle alight. Sir Vivian sat unmoved at the spectacle, only when the alien breeze wafted great clouds of smoke in his direction did he come to life. His whole frame shook as he coughed and spluttered, he rubbed his eyes as the fumes stung and discomforted them. It was then that Margaret stepped in between him and the smoke. Her timing had always been good. She spoke as Sir Vivian choked.

'I know it's a liberty, sir, but I must speak. The defending garrison is out making skirmish attacks on Fascists. It seems they have been outflanked and the hospital is outflanked by the enemy.'

Sir Vivian gazed at Margaret as though she were a new dawn, she helped the awakening on its way by shrieking.

'Outflanked, sir, outflanked!'

He rose to his feet and staggered towards her.

'What's a woman doing here?' he muttered.

'I am a nurse, sir. This comes before my womanhood, before my sexual gender. And you, sir, are a soldier before you are a man, we are both in the course of duty. Let us not forget it.'

'Quite so, nurse, quite so', said Sir Vivian drawing himself to attention. Margaret wrung her hands in anguish.

'Oh, sir, what can one soldier do against fifty. How can you help us? I can manage the enemy within, but. . . .'

'The enemy within?' Sir Vivian asked hoarsely.

Margaret nodded her head and pushed a convenient wisp of hair from her brow as a welcome tear trickled down her left cheek.

'My God, not . . . not cholera?'

'Worse', said Margaret.

Sir Vivian listened with attentive dread totally alive for the next catastrophe that was to come.

'Scabies', she said.

'Scabies', gasped Sir Vivian.

'Probably brought in by Fascist spies and planted in the officers' wards – only the officers are infected, the men seem to be clear. I suppose the aim was to skim off our cream. We must conserve our water supplies for sulphur baths, but it has been necessary to burn the linen.'

They both looked at the remains of the smouldering rags and Sir Vivian's voice shook with emotion as he spoke.

'Leave the outside to me, madam. The heart of England will not be destroyed by pestilence under the skin, nor without it.'

He scanned the garden with a military eye.

'Trenches and dynamite will do the trick.'

Margaret was a little worried about Sir Vivian immediately embarking on such a heavy physical task.

'Shall we draw up contingency plans over lunch, sir?'

The pending battle had titillated all Sir Vivian's senses and he acquiesced to Margaret's suggestion with Napoleonic deference. He took her arm and escorted her to the kitchen, it would have been difficult for an outside observer to know which one was supporting the other, such was the subtlety of Margaret's art.

Differing strategies were discussed over bread, cheese, tomatoes and tea. The conversation was friendly, but rigidly professional.

'I realise the need for the trenches, but tell me, sir, how can you ignite the dynamite without laying yourself open to injury? Forgive my forwardness, sir, but to place your life in abeyance would be tantamount to placing us all at risk here.'

Sir Vivian took another stab of Cheddar and answered Margaret as he sliced the cheese.

'A good question, madam, and forcibly put. Fortunately, we have quantities of fuse and it will be possible for me to implement detonation from the safety of the main building. Quite simply, the answer to your question is adequate preparation, a formidable prospect you might say, but not an impossible one.'

Margaret nodded, and thought of the other mounds of moulding linen lying around the upstairs of the house.

'I must burn the rest of the infected sheets, perhaps this activity would possibly screen your digging objectives from snipers.'

'Excellent, excellent idea', retorted Sir Vivian. 'But tell me, madam, how are these utensils to be replaced? A cold bed is no place for a soldier to sleep, least of all an officer.'

Margaret took a huge bite of cheese and tomato to give herself time to think – a lady never spoke whilst she was eating. The food gave her valuable time for respite. She answered gravely.

'I believe, sir, you have read the recent instructions on military survival. Section thirty-three follows the piece on food rationing during times of invasion, or occupation. It is usually overlooked as it deals with Arctic conditions and clothing resources. It will probably come as a surprise to you that the human body generates as much heat as three blankets. I have alerted my nurses with regard to the seriousness of the situation and I am glad to say that they are all prepared, without exception, to answer the call of duty. The only alternative would be to ask the men to move into the officers' quarters. I am sure that you would agree on the inadvisability of the secondary alternative.'

Sir Vivian drained his tea.

'I take my hat off to you, madam, and your good sisters. What about numbers?'

'There are eleven officers and eight nurses.'

'Oh!'

'Fortunately, one of the nurses has liberal inclinations and is of ample physical proportions – she will manage the two cadet officers. I myself, also intend to set an example so you need have no fears for the nocturnal dangers which might otherwise have assailed your corps.'

Margaret proffered more tea, but Sir Vivian ended the meeting by sighing and said,

'It has been a pleasure meeting you, madam, and now, if you will excuse me, I have some digging to do.'

An hour later Margaret persuaded the old soldier to take some rest from his toil. She escorted him into his study and tempted him with a little fruit cake as he sat propped up in one of the large armchairs. He was asleep before he had finished eating the cake. She took the unfinished slice from his hand and gently brushed away the morsels that had clung to his whiskers. His snoring gave her added satisfaction and triumph. He won't die she thought, and then drew the curtains, quietly as only a real nurse could.

It was sad that Margaret had never been socially trained to acquire a taste for coffee. At least, she put it down to social training as no one could imagine how much she loathed the taste of it. Even the aroma from the stuff sickened her. She believed that people that drank it did not really like it. Yet in London, they seemed to absorb its flavour in every shape and form. E.B.-J. had left the 'Melair' box of coffee-cream chocolates on the table for Margaret's benefit.

'Give yourself a little time with them, adjust yourself to eating without tasting. It's quite simple, think of oranges while they are in your mouth.'

This was good advice, as Margaret was due, later in the week, to present this particular coffee delight to a new public. Nevertheless, she viewed the coffee-orange chocolates before her with dread, she took one from the box.

'This is my medicine. It will make me better, it will cure my leukaemia, anaemia, and septicaemia. I am happy to eat it.'

Thinking this way, her brain managed to force her jaws open for no less than three chocolates, she even managed a wan smile as she chewed her way through the third one. A fourth chocolate was dropped on to the floor before the cure was complete as a piercing scream rang through the house. It had come from the garden.

Wintner was standing just inside the garden gate when Margaret reached him, he appeared to be looking into his shopping bags which had fallen into disarray near his feet.

'Are you all right?' he asked.

'Yes', said Margaret somewhat breathlessly.

'Of course, I'm all right', another voice came from nowhere. 'Is that you, Margaret? Did you manage to eat any of the coffee-creams?'

Margaret moved forward.

'Careful', said Wintner and pointed as he spoke.

Margaret observed E.B.-J. whose head was just visible behind the bags. The first victim of trench warfare was calmly adjusting her bun into its correct position on top of her head. Margaret looked down at her.

126

'Yes, I ate three. It's a good job they're not detonated.'

'Detonated?' said Wintner.

'The trenches. Sir Vivian thought of them this afternoon. He has talked, eaten, and now he's sleeping.'

'You've done well, miss', said Wintner.

'She's most competent at whatever she does', said E.B.-J. as Margaret and Wintner hauled her to eye-level. The dust on her clothing did not seem to bother her, but Margaret's uniform gave her momentary concern.

'Are you hurt, my love?' Margaret was taken aback by E.B.-J.'s tenderness and the sudden lack of composure declared on her behalf.

'Oh, no, I'm not hurt, it's ketchup. It was all part of the game, part of the cure.'

She caught the relief on both their faces and felt quietly gratified. The three of them walked slowly to the house linked together by shopping bags.

'He'll want to continue this campaign tomorrow', said Wintner.

'We can't let him detonate the garden', said Margaret.

'Yes we can', said E.B.-J. as they entered the kitchen. 'Give him celery, it should do well here and I'm partial to it.'

'Yes, celery that's it. Celery', said Wintner. 'I'll get some dinner for us, you've saved his life, miss.'

'She's done that for all of us, Harry', said E.B.-J. 'I'm going to change my clothes.'

Margaret left to answer the telephone which had just commenced ringing.

The voice was quiet, soft, with a mild trace of a London accent. Only actors spoke 'Cockney'.

'I can see you on Wednesday, you're down for a centre piece on the coffee-cream thing. Perhaps we could eat together?'

It was the technician speaking.

'I've thought about you a lot since I last saw you. Is your name . . .', he paused. 'Is your name really Trixie?'

'I don't know', said Margaret truthfully. 'I honestly don't know who I am. I suppose I will one day. It's quite important that I should know. Your name is Duncan, I heard some of the others calling it. Tell me about your teeth.'

He chuckled.

'Well they are all my own.'

'No I want a little more information than that. Could you explain the formation.'

He answered defensively, he hadn't expected a dental analysis.

'My teeth are just ordinary, a few fillings here and there, but nothing much wrong with them.'

'Oh!' Margaret sighed with disappointment.

'Except, excepting one thing which some say is unusual, some say is lucky.'

Margaret's interest rekindled as he continued.

'My two front teeth have a space between them.'

'I knew it, I knew it. Could you get a sixpence between the space?' her voice quavered.

'I suppose so, at a push, I've never tried. I can whistle through them for you if you'll agree to meet.'

He laughed again, more from bewilderment than anything else.

'There's no need to whistle, Duncan', said Margaret quietly. 'I'm just beginning to wait for Wednesday which means I'm waiting to see you.'

'You're funny', he said.

'I'll see you Wednesday', she murmured as he began whistling down the telephone.

The roast lamb was very good that evening and the company even better. Wintner prepared and presented food as though he were invisible, no effort seemed required and any help offered in the process of preparation received a cold, polite, rebuttal. Sir Vivian had chosen to leave his room and eat with the rest of the household. This he had not done for many years.

E.B.-J. wore a deep crimson housecoat for the occasion, the top four buttons were left unfastened, she had abandoned her bun and her thick dark hair hung loosely about her shoulders. Sir Vivian excused himself immediately after dinner because of urgent business that he was forced to attend to in the library.

'I hate to leave the family at such a time, but I know you will understand.'

'Family?' Margaret questioned the word.

'Yes, nice isn't it?' said E.B.-J.

They all agreed that it was.

'Do you think we should marry, Stella?' said Wintner as E.B.-J. tied the top of his pyjama trousers. Her evening's pleasure and early morning awakening complete, she sat up in bed, pushed her fingers through her hair and thought about the proposal.

'No, I don't think there's any need. If you do what we are doing at eighteen it's considered wrong and lots of people get upset. If you do it at forty or over, the same people would be indifferent. We are both at the stage where this sort of thing is only important to us. At seventy, people will be glad to see us together, we will be termed companions.'

This unemotional declaration of future intent gave Wintner more reassurance than a register office.

'We won't be just companions at seventy', he said as he pulled E.B.-J. into a horizontal position.

An hour later E.B.-J. was re-tying his pyjamas.

'I believe you', she said.

'I'll wake Margaret and make some breakfast. You make me so happy, Stella', he said.

She gurgled and sang a little (a most unusual thing for her to do) on her way to the bathroom. The pointer on the scales gave her momentary disquiet. She had gained five pounds in less than a fortnight and was having a slight problem in coaxing the zip of her navy-blue skirt into its closed position over her bottom. A sharp intake of breath finally organised her clothing for the day which was to be a busy one. Margaret had agreed to do some typing before going on to Shepherds Bush; what a strange girl she had turned out to be; separate from everyone, still an orphan. Her bosom rose as she thought of the girl. I love her too. No need to prove it to her, she would find out some time, she was no fool. E.B.-J. left for the office in a hurry. She failed to notice the letter addressed to her in green biro as she rushed past the hall-table. Loving, one way or another, had left her a little vague rather than forgetful. This increased her efficiency as priorities were dealt with first and the innumerable hysterical and petty demands which had formerly immobilised her emotionally, now left her unscathed and becalmed.

They had managed to find a workmen's café near the studio. It was painted inside and out, cream and green, with a layer of grease. The place was so busy and active that it left them completely private. There was a small scar positioned almost directly on his temple; it was white and it stood out like a little crescent moon on his brow. Margaret's eyes wandered from the scar to his teeth as he spoke. He caught her eye movements and frowned.

'I suppose you are nervous about the shooting. Don't worry, everyone thought that you were great at rehearsal.'

He squeezed her knee under the table, withdrew his hand and then pressed one of her legs between his knees and held her in a gentle vice.

'I'm not nervous about the filming', said Margaret anxiously. 'It's the coffee-creams, I can't bear them, not even the smell, let alone the taste. They make me sick.'

She placed her hands on the table and leaned forward. He was laughing at her. She frowned and leaned across towards him.

'Funny is it?' she snapped, her chin jutting forward in irritation.

Then he surprised her by covering her small hands with his own and enveloping her whole mouth, lips, teeth and tongue within his. Her legs encased, her hands trapped, she thought no more of imprisonment as his mouth persuaded her into willing submission.

'Two bacon sandwiches.' The call from the counter of the crowded café seemed to bounce back from the large steamed-up mirror on the opposite wall. The sandwiches waited.

'Two bacon sandwiches, counter-service only', shrieked the elderly female assistant who took her work very seriously.

One of the workmen gently tapped Margaret on the shoulder and she and Duncan withdrew from the centre of the table to their respective seats, both breathing heavily. The noise of the café had abated. It was then that Margaret realised that she had an audience that she had not bargained for. Embarrassed, Duncan offered her a cigarette, they both heard the match strike.

'Your sandwiches', whispered the man who had tapped Margaret's shoulder.

She jumped up quickly and travelled like a nun with averted eyes to collect them from the counter.

'Sauce is on the tables, but I don't think you need any, dear', rasped the counterhand.

Loud guffaws broke the quiet, the place then resumed its comfortable disorder and Margaret and Duncan ate their sandwiches in peace, leaving unnoticed, passion savoured but unspent.

He held her arm tightly and guided her into the confectioner's. 'Ten boxes of peppermint-creams, please', he said. 'No one can know what's inside the coating.'

She smiled, accepting the gentle ambiguity.

'I like peppermint', she said.

'You might not after the session, you can have too much of anything.' So saying he ushered her back to the studio where once more she prepared herself to represent the ranks of downtrodden womanhood.

The filmed sequence showed that 'Melair' coffee-creams could (if administered by a husband popping them into a wife's mouth as though it were a letter box) save her from manic depression, or mental breakdown. The breakdown had ensued because of the said spouse's long hours spent at the office away from the family nook in Surbiton. The poor housewife appeared to spend the whole day waiting for his return; each extra minute after six signified a step nearer towards a total emotional collapse. Fortunately, before this was finalised, the errant husband arrived and cared for her completely by feeding her as though she were a goldfish followed by big smiles and a quick shot of marital bliss. The chocolates, if taken at filmed value, could have made all forms of psychiatric care redundant within a year. The two-minute sequence took all day to film and only one box of coffee creams was left after completion. Margaret felt sick, but did not vomit. Perhaps the effect of the cheque for £110 had helped settle her stomach.

She had expected him to walk her to the bus-stop, or even see her home. He had said, 'I will telephone, is that all right?' She nodded and managed a wan smile. His intentions were less serious than she had thought them to be. It was odd how urgent men could get over sex, it was a bit like diarrhoea with them. It couldn't be helped, but it was almost a relief when it was over. But then, in this case, it hadn't happened anyway. She gave the remaining box of chocolates to a talkative old lady in the bus queue, half-hoping that the gesture might eliminate the woman's chatter and her own preoccupations with Duncan. The old woman continued to prattle even more. Margaret half listened, her stomach felt very queasy, not on account of the quantity of peppermint-cream it had absorbed, for the queasiness swept right through her body. She arrived in Bayswater rumbling with desire. It obviously affected women too, arriving home she felt most disconnected and uncomfortable.

'It's silly, I don't even know him', she thought sensibly. Unfortunately, she was still prone to intermittent rumblings.

Uncharacteristically, she found E.B.-J. slumped on a chair in the kitchen with her head buried in both hands. A torn envelope lay on the table and its contents, two pages of green biro, had fallen on the floor beside her. She gathered the pages together and made an effort for Margaret.

'They were very pleased. . . .'

'What's wrong?' asked Margaret. She wished to share her friend's anguish.

E.B.-J. was absolved of the niceties and formalities peculiar to ordinary greeting; true friends could always waive them at such times.

'It's from my sister. Very bad news, very bad indeed.'

She shook her head and paused, placing the letter on the table before her.

'I am required to send a considerable amount of money to her in order that she can acquire temporary freedom. She requests a loan of £500 so that she can be released on bail.'

'Released?' She's caged, thought Margaret, caged.

'Apparently, she is to stand trial on 27 February next year. The charge is not a pleasant one. Quite serious in fact. Blackmail.'

She spoke the word quietly and lit a cigarette. She pointed to the letter.

'It must have arrived this morning, I never noticed until I got home. Of course, I shall make arrangements to have the

money forwarded immediately. I am very sorry that you have
to be involved in all this. . . .'

'Me?'

'She asks us all to attend court on the twenty-seventh, me,
Wintner and you.'

'I don't understand', said Margaret.

E.B.-J. sighed and made a gesture for Margaret to read the
letter, she leaned back in her chair as Margaret unfolded the
pages. Before she looked at the pages, Margaret received a nod
of assurance from E.B.-J., apparently she did not feel that anything private was under threat.

7 Cloisterswalk,
Wolhamthorpe,
Framptonshire.
Date as Post Mark.

Dear Stella,

How lovely Autumn is this year, all red and gold, it is
always a season so full of surprises. Keats did not give
true justice to it all, if only Chekov had been English, or
Keats had been a Socialist, something satisfactory might
have captured the essence of it all. As it is, we have to be
satisfied with our own impressions and as yours are a
little limited in the sensuous creative aspects of observation,
I am jogging them a bit with mine. Sisters we are, and if
we can't compensate each other in little ways, then the
brotherhood of man will never come. And this I will never
believe. Although, I am at times dismayed by the
ingratitude of my fellow-beings, at the moment, I am a
victim of such ingratitude and that is why I am writing.
For the past eight months I have been employed as an
emotional counsellor to the Head of the local Technical
College here. It has been quite the most demanding and
exhausting position that I have ever held. I will not tire
you with the intricacies and bothersome details which I
have been subjected to in the course of my work, but I can

assure you that the payment for my labour (which has taken a great personal toll of me) has been pitiful.

Margaret looked up from the page. 'Lena is. . . .'
'My sister. My older sister', said E.B.-J.
Margaret's eyes returned to the letter as Wintner entered and took up one of his favoured positions standing just behind E.B.-J.'s chair. Lena's voice crept from the pages into Margaret's head.

For the first time in my life, I was forced by circumstances to ask for some kind of remuneration as part payment for many duties and tasks which I had undertaken without sanction or complaint. Imagine my shock and horror when two gentlemen in dirty raincoats called on me and informed me that I was being charged with no less than blackmail. I will not bore you with the ensuing interviews at the police station and solicitors' offices. I am to appear at Wolhamthorpe Court on the 27th of February of next year falsely charged with blackmail. I view this interview without trepidation as my recent experience has taught me that the law is nothing but a game of snakes and ladders bearing little relevance to justice. If the dice are in my favour, I will not have to enter the charade as in the past I have known two of the circuit judges and I am sure that both will remain loyal to me if the case is allocated to them.

In the meantime, my dear, I wonder if you would forward fivehundred pounds to my solicitors, Pangland & Co., High Street, Wolhamthorpe. Part of the money releases me on bail and part of it pays for fripperies which they call defence. I would like you to accompany me in court on the day, please bring Margaret and Harry with you. If my forecasts are right all three of you will now be much happier for knowing one another and I am not ashamed of claiming responsibility for it. No doubt, you will have gathered by now that Margaret is above the 'herd' – she is fixed outside of time, matter and space – of star quality. She should know of this letter, this episode will add further to her training.

Writing is a false means of communication, I have always favoured the spoken word myself, next to these are thoughts, and in this respect, all three of you are ever in my mind. Knowing that kinship and cherished memories can never be torn or broken by absence or event, I await your swift reply.

Ever, Lena.

P.S. Perhaps, it would be as well if you made contact with my solicitors immediately.

Margaret handed the letter to Wintner, she felt as though she had just completed a drama class.

'I've never been inside a court of law in my life, Lena doesn't seem worried by it all.'

'She's not, worry is beneath her', said E.B.-J.

'I like her', said Margaret defensively.

'So do I, the bitch. We all like her', said E.B.-J. She sighed and continued.

'You don't have to come with us, Margaret, it could be a ghastly ordeal.'

'I want to come', said Margaret prompted more by curiosity than compassion.

Wintner dropped the letter into E.B.-J.'s lap and quickly organised himself into preparing runner-beans for the evening meal. He worked with undue haste slashing the beans in half so that more food fell into the waste-bin than into the saucepan of water. The two ladies waited for the carnage to abate, but it was not until he had slaughtered all of the beans that he finally managed to speak.

'Ahem, ahem, of course I am not able to leave Sir Vivian here on his own. I have to balance my accountability. . . .'

'Sir Vivian could accompany us, the journey would be good for him', said E.B.-J. in a dry voice.

'Oh, he wouldn't contemplate such a thing', Wintner placed the beans on the stove.

'I could persuade him to come, we could make an adventure of it', said Margaret.

'Your presumptions are arrogant, miss, if I may say so. Arrogant', snapped Wintner as he turned his back on both of them. Margaret felt injured and E.B.-J. rose from her chair and adjusted her bun.

'Harry'. She waited for him to turn. It was necessary for her to address him in forthright almost cruel tones.

'Harry.' He turned, she spoke. 'Please sit down, thank you. You are afraid to come with us. You are afraid to travel to Wolhamthorpe. We will accept the truth, but speak it.'

'Me afraid of the law and born and bred in Dalston, afraid of a court. No, duty is duty, Stella, and I know where my responsibilities lie – here.'

This seemed fair enough to Margaret, but E.B.-J. was not mollified. She took a carrot from his hands, relieved him of the paring knife and nipped off the root and stalk and let them drop on to the kitchen floor.

'Yes, they are sisters; the likeness is quite marked', thought Margaret.

'Not afraid of the law, Harry?' E.B.-J.'s voice took on a derelict, sad quality; she stroked his head and let her palm rest on the back of his neck.

'Not afraid of the court?' she whispered. 'Afraid of her; afraid of her, aren't you?'

He looked up to her and then buried his head in her belly; she began to stroke his hair. He did not need to speak.

'Oh dear,' said Margaret, but did not say more as E.B.-J. began to talk reverently, quietly, without expression, almost as though she were taking part in some strange litany.

'It's a question of choice, Harry; it's just as it was in Dalston twenty years ago. I won't compete with Lena, I can't, you know that. We offer something different and you have to choose.'

138

Wintner groaned. 'I won't see her.'

'It's no good, Harry, I must know. There is no sense in you being with me if there is a single thought for her; see her and you might be free of her, if you're not, then. . . .'

Wintner groaned. E.B.-J. spoke.

'You want to see her, you do, don't you?'

'Yes, I want to see her', gasped Wintner and stood clasping E.B.-J. to him. 'I want to see her.'

Sir Vivian's voice parted them as it rang from the study.

'Margaret, Margaret, my dear. Did you remember to get the leather?'

'Y-e-s, four pieces, each a yard square, I have bought a punch too. They are in the hall, under the stair cupboard.'

Mutterings of appreciation came from the hall-way, E.B.-J. and Wintner cast quizzical glances in Margaret's direction, Margaret was grateful for the diversion.

'They are for catapults Sir Vivian is assembling across some of the window frames; from what he says I gather that they will be able to fire a hundred yards with great accuracy. All approaches to the house can be covered quite easily.'

Wintner had returned to the stove.

'There can't be much force to them.'

E.B.-J. had begun to recover a little. Margaret hastened the recovery touching E.B.-J.'s shoulder as she left the room.

'Oh, yes, we can muster quite a bit of force, quite a lot of power', she paused. 'That's if we all pull together.'

E.B.-J. patted Margaret's hand. Strong allies were difficult to come by.

It was possible to travel for miles and miles and still be in London. Margaret had discovered this for herself since meeting Duncan. He lived in Forest Gate which meant journeying by Tube and electric rail. Each time she took the journey, it seemed to be further away than the time before. She had known him for thirteen weeks now, just over. She pondered over this as the train braked for its first stop after leaving Liverpool Street Station. A howling wind blew heavy rain against the windows of the carriage, condensation inside made the panes redundant. It didn't matter. She knew the scenery, every estate, each tiny factory or shed. She no longer felt the need to look or wonder. She looked at her watch, 8.30 a.m., we must be at Hackney Downs, five more stops. They met only in the mornings; the evenings belonged to his wife who was a social worker. He was very fond of his wife and did not want her hurt.

The situation and the arrangements surrounding it left Margaret in a constant state of ache. They had said goodbye often, saying 'it was better that way' and Margaret had felt noble and good for two days. After which, she prayed for the 'phone call; if he did not call, then she did. The forced estrangements merely heightened their passion. Happiness did not enter it at all and when Margaret stepped from the train into the driving rain, she welcomed it. Christmas was always depicted with seasonal snow. Not a trace in sight, the morning light, dark and dreary, suited the present landscape. In spite of this, she hurried to the semi-detached house – rushing towards the few hours of ecstasy which fed and nurtured her present state of despair.

'You're soaked to the skin', he said as he helped her from her coat.

'Come into the kitchen, it's warmer there. Let me have your shoes and socks, I'll dry them for you. Look, you're shivering.'

His tender, almost feminine, concern about small details of well-being always left her helpless. It dispelled any cynicism or rancour that she might muster in allaying her feelings, or love, for him. It made the partings more brutal in that he was gentle.

Their love-making contradicted the sweetness. They undressed, looked at each other under the harsh neon light of the kitchen. Orgasms were shared on the chequered linoleum, over chairs, pinioned across the table. Exploration that left no contours or blemishes untouched by taste or touch left them exhausted. Margaret's journeys through these deserts of love found no oasis. Today, as always, they sat holding one another. She looked in the fold behind his right ear lobe for the blackhead that she hoped might repel her. It was still there. She kissed the ear gently and he placed his hand on her where she was wet and sore.

'I'll roll us a cigarette', he said.

It always had to be re-lit two or three times and it always signified that it was nearly time to dress. The cigarette was a substitute for sleep; the proximity of the afterwards of love was slender, and these moments Margaret savoured most of all. He leaned back and inhaled deeply before passing the roll-up to Margaret. He spoke as he handed it to her.

'She knows.'

Margaret paused, the roll-up had died.

'Pardon?' she asked weakly.

'Sheila, Sheila, my wife, she knows. I told her', he said.

Margaret was suddenly aware of draughts and pulled her cardigan around her shoulders. She rested her head across his knee.

'Is she angry?'

He shook his head.

'I suppose she's too upset at the moment', said Margaret.

He rose and began to dress.

'No. She doesn't seem upset either. In fact, she is being very fair. I had to tell her. I mean, it couldn't go on like this. I've tried to call it a day often enough, but I have to see you and each time we hurt each other all the more. When I told her I just said that I had to be with you.'

Margaret fastened the back of her dress.

'You mean you want to live with me?'

'Yes, I suppose so.'

They held each other and nuzzled like cow and calf. He continued.

'She feels we should all talk it over together. It might be a good idea if you brought a friend with you, this was her idea.'

'I don't know what we can talk about. What I feel is private', said Margaret.

'She wants us to meet here next Saturday at two – don't worry please. Will you come – for me?' he asked wading through her bewilderment.

'All right', she said.

He collected her shoes which were drying under the radiator, she noticed the camouflaged glance at his watch. It was odd how wounding such minor duplicities were to her. She winced and covered her injury by a swift departure to the bathroom.

'I must go now then', she stood in the eau-de-nil decorated hall-way and fixed her eyes on the Picasso print (blue period) which hung in copied compassion just inside the door. He kissed her on the nose.

'Who's going to look after you?' he muttered.

She squeezed his arm and slipped away quietly. She did not turn but heard the click on the catch of the door as it closed behind her. She pushed her socks deep into her pockets, they were still damp.

The signals had delayed her train; fortunately the rain had paused. Waiting did not help her. She tried not to think of him, but images crowded her mind with the insistence of a pneumatic drill. When she was not with him, this was how it was, she imagined what he might be doing. This had reached an absurd level to the point where she was wondering if he liked jam-tarts, and if so, which did he prefer, apricot or raspberry, when fortunately the train arrived.

E.B.-J. tugged fiercely at the hydrangeas. She had never liked them. Since selling her maisonette in Beckenham, she felt that she never wanted to look at them ever again. Here in Bayswater they appeared as bossy as ever, just the same as rhododendrons. Give them a chance to flower and they took over everything, blocking light and shade from all other growing things. If ignored, they became larger and greedier year by year so that there was nothing left after a time, but a garden of blue and pink lumps of paper-like froth. She pulled at a second clump, digging her heels into the ground. Her hands slid along the tough shiny stalks, she fell back clutching three blooms. The plant remained in the earth, bald and defiant. Her bottom which had continued to widen in recent weeks, preserved her from injury, but glancing towards the pathway to her left, she saw that a small figure had witnessed her indignity. It looked more like a pagoda than anything else. Two black flared trouser legs were capped by a cone-like cloak of orange and yellow. The tiny feet were clamped in red clogs and a long neck plus a small agile face framed in red-rinsed curls, provided the apparition with a weather vane. It turned north-east towards her. E.B.-J. was always pleased to see Margaret.

She looked again at the girl who now sat on the window ledge near her. The brown-shadowed eyes that stared emptily ahead took on the appearance of large prunes. The overlapped leg had kicked off its clog to reveal one big toe nail painted green, the rest of the toes were left to nature.

'You'll catch cold going about barefoot in this weather', said E.B.-J. as she handed the tops of the flowers to Margaret.

The girl did not answer, but slid her foot back into the clog. E.B.-J. joined her on the ledge.

'His wife knows', said Margaret emptily. 'I have to meet her next Saturday. She wants a discussion.'

The prunes had begun to moisten so that the liberal application of eye shadow and mascara widened in circumference, an ear-ring had left its mooring and E.B.-J. looked into the face of a tragic, lop-sided female clown. The mask was real enough and hid nothing.

'He says I can bring a friend with me.'

'Me', said E.B.-J.

They walked towards the house.

'I left the flowers on the window ledge', said Margaret and half-turned to fetch them.

E.B.-J. restrained her gently.

'Leave them', she said. 'There's nothing to them, nothing at all to them.'

Margaret's emotional state did not stop her from answering the demands of her vocation. Unlike most girls in her chosen profession, she could not undertake all the calls on her time for the particular skills that she had to offer. E.B.-J. requested more for her services, but this did not deter the three companies who provided an arduous week's work. 'Heartsease Margarine',

'Landscape Cigarettes', and a vaginal spray which was supposed to leave her confident and fresh, all added a great deal to her bank balance and kept her working until after seven most evenings. What was left of each evening was spent mainly with Sir Vivian who interspersed their little charades with,

'Do not let them destroy you' or 'You have always got your rear-guard.'

Wintner pampered her with food and E.B.-J. was just there.

Somehow, Saturday arrived and Margaret was still alive.

Sheila Livingstone placed nine pieces of shortbread on a decorated plate, three tea bags in the empty tea-pot and two roses in the small narrow vase on the table. She had dispatched Duncan to the hardware shop – one of the taps needed a new washer. This gave her half-an-hour to herself to contemplate the afternoon ahead of her.

She enjoyed a challenge. This was one of the reasons that had persuaded her to become a social worker. In the past three years she had progressed far; she was now an area team leader. This was more enjoyable than working in the field as she enjoyed nothing more than appraising what other people had done. She was becoming an expert on leading discussions. If one discussed long enough, it was easy enough to get one's way as people forgot to make decisions, or had to leave to attend to the shopping. She was always understanding about family pressures. She thought of the eyes of the new trainee who had stared at her in admiration before she had left the office that morning.

'Dorothy my dear, I forbid you to visit that family this weekend. I know three days without gas or electricity won't be pleasant, but remember, our job is to teach people to help themselves, not breast-feed them day and night. You have to wean them from you. I know it sounds harsh, but I am thinking of both you and them. Now off you go and we will organise your concern on Monday.'

The girl had left as though papally blessed. Sheila smiled with satisfaction and turned the gas from medium to full as the day began to freeze.

In spite of the cold, she decided not to change from the ankle-length black cotton dress which was sweetly speckled with green and white daisies. Her hair, worn shoulder-length, was parted directly down the middle and well brushed. Small nose, small green eyes and a tiny mouth emphasised the sweetness which she was at pains to convey. Only a trace of make-up freshened the rather sallow complexion which was almost the colour of the pale green daisies on her dress. The prospect of the afternoon meeting sent ripples of controlled excitement through her body.

Poor Duncan, this had happened twice before and each time it only made him realise how much he really loved her and depended on her. After the first girl – some chit of a manageress at The British Home Stores – she had paid for six months' analysis for him and that had finished it off. The second one nose-dived after some marriage counselling with her friend Dr Jean Standling, who had clearly pointed out to Duncan that his dallying with Edna was no more than a yearning for pre-adolescent masturbation. Through all of this, Sheila had remained sweetly forgiving.

Now that she was a qualified social worker, an area team leader, she felt that she was quite competent in dealing with this new girl herself. Trixie, the name was more suitable for a bitch. She stopped herself from laughing aloud as she heard Duncan's key in the door and adopted a face of gentle gravity more befitting the terms of reference adopted for the afternoon's agenda.

The guests arrived on time. Formalities of introduction were brutally swift and all four were seated with tea and shortbreads within five minutes of encounter. Sheila opened the meeting.

'You probably won't believe me, but I am pleased to meet you.' She passed a piece of shortbread to Margaret. 'Really pleased – you can dip if you like.'

'Pardon?' asked Margaret as she held the shortbread as if it were a frog or a beetle.

Sheila smiled and continued, 'Your shortbread, dear, dip it in your tea if you like, I want you to feel at home, comfortable. Just do and say what you feel.'

She pushed her hair gently away from her face and turned to Duncan who had cast his eyes down at the table and looked more like a cocker-spaniel than a man.

'After all, that is why we are here. It's essential for us to be relaxed if we are going to get at the truth of all this.'

'I don't dip', said Margaret.

E.B.-J.'s expression remained unchanged, but she adjusted her hair bun which was already perfectly placed. Duncan's head sank lower into his chest.

'A good opening', thought Sheila.

'It seems that all of us are unhappy and saddened by the present situation. I don't see any point in laying blame, or in exchanging recriminations. It seems to me that we should really examine our individual needs.'

She sipped her tea.

'Needs?' Margaret asked vacantly.

'Mm-m-mm', noised Sheila as she swallowed a soggy piece of shortbread. 'A painful process for us all, but we must try to see why Duncan felt the need for you, why you felt the need

148

for him, and why I felt the need for this to occur. You see, one could say that I had unconsciously manoeuvred this débàcle.'

E.B.-J. frowned. She disliked the woman and found it impossible to drink the tea in front of her. Sheila mistook her expression for one of puzzlement rather than distaste. She smiled briskly in her direction and continued, 'Yes, although blame should not enter it, I feel that I am totally responsible for us all being here.'

'That's obvious, you invited us', Margaret spoke aggressively.

Sheila's studied calm worked well.

'No, dear. I mean that I am responsible for you knowing Duncan. More tea?'

Margaret shook her head, provoked further, her irritation increased.

'He pursued me alone, he must have needed me to have done that. I didn't answer an advertisement.' Her voice rose. 'I was not on the market.'

E.B.-J. laid a restraining hand on Margaret and looked to Duncan for help. His face had the look of St Sebastian in that his agony was no longer of this earth. He offered no help.

'You are right', said Sheila who offered a sad, understanding smile to her husband as she spoke. 'He did pursue you; I asked him to.'

'What?' asked E.B.-J.

'Not directly, of course, but subconsciously I asked – no demanded – that my husband should seek out another woman. I am not surprised that it is you. I can see that you are a young, attractive, lively girl that could give him a lot of attention. You must believe me when I say that I am grateful to you.'

Margaret tried to suppress the waves of nausea and anger that clouded her thoughts; she had arrived thinking that her own guilt would make her compassionate rather than jealous. She felt neither. The more she looked and listened, the more she felt convinced that she was involved in a rescue operation for Duncan's personal survival than in a decision for his continuing love.

'You're killing him.' Margaret could not expand on this. E.B.-J. understood and Sheila didn't seem to hear.

'Yes, grateful, I have been so busy trying to meet the needs of others in the course of my work that I have overlooked the needs of the one closest to me.' She gave Duncan yet another understanding smile.

'The needs of others?' E.B.-J. was puzzled.

'I am a social worker.' Sheila paused and waited hopefully for some words of encouragement which would lead her into her favourite themes of caring and committal. The silence did not put her off. She looked beyond Margaret and E.B.-J. and spoke reverently of her profession.

'I have felt that I should offer a personal service to my clients, although I am working for the state. Caring needs to be organised and the only way to help anyone is to get them to help themselves.'

E.B.-J. cracked Sheila's composure.

'You are paid to care?' she asked. She was genuinely curious. 'How do you manage to apportion it? I would have thought it should be spontaneous.'

'Training, coupled with experience, does lend one extra insights, but I feel we are straying a little.'

Sheila sensed danger from the older woman. The meeting would not have to be as long as she had originally planned it to be. Duncan had almost become attentive; he had never questioned the integrity of the female saint that he had chosen to marry. He glanced covertly in E.B.-J.'s direction, but it was no more than a glance. For some reason he was afraid of meeting Margaret's gaze. Sheila's voice sounded less real than ever.

'The emotional and physical side of our marriage has always been sound, but you know, domesticity is not without passion. Interests became either mutual or more intensely singular. It is in the question of interests where I have failed my husband.'

Margaret gritted her teeth. 'My husband' – did that mean property? Did it mean ownership? Perhaps it did, perhaps that is what a wedding was all about, a term of purchase like a house conveyance.

'He has always been ready to listen to the painstaking details of my work, always been sympathetic to the intricacies and nuances of human foibles and relationships. I can't blame him for this, as a camera can only mirror and not observe. We have discussed this and that is why we came to a mutual conclusion, which, whilst it might be initially painful, would resolve our present difficulties.'

'Yours, his, or mine?' Margaret spoke quietly, numbed by the arrogance of the woman.

'All, all of us will benefit, my dear. In time you'll be able to breathe retrospective sighs of thanks. We have concentrated on his work prospects rather than mine and he is taking up a position in a large automobile factory. Essentially, his role will emerge as a technical adviser to all their photography and advertising sections. In this context, he will have to be account-able to all kinds of pressures. Eventually it will probably lead to a managerial post.'

Sheila paused for a moment and philosophised. 'Account-ability is not a bad thing you know. Of course, it will mean moving into Essex. Commuting will mean a little sacrifice on my part, but I have considered that and am prepared to make it.'

Margaret spoke to Duncan directly, ignoring Sheila.

'But you want to go into filming, you want to make things for yourself – you have ideas and. . . .'

He shook his head slowly. Margaret's words withered.

'Duncan is an idealist, I would not take these from him, but a functional idealist is more truly idealistic than a dreamer. His work will be a therapy and this means recovery and change. It seems sensible to me that we all make our adieux now with as little hysteria as possible.'

Sheila stood and placed an arm round her husband's shoulders. He in turn lifted a heavy arm and let it rest on her waist. E.B.-J. collected the coats from the hall and helped Margaret to dress for the cold. Sheila saw them to the door.

'No further contact then?' She spoke brightly.

'No', said Margaret.

Sheila looked to E.B.-J.

'I know you will help in all this.'

Margaret had reached the pavement and E.B.-J. lingered a while before the door closed. She met Sheila's gaze.

'No further contact, I will agree to that. I am worried for you. It's more than likely you may contaminate others besides your husband. It's very sad that your disease is not classifiable.'

For a second, Sheila lost her composure, but recovered it sufficiently to be able to close the door quietly.

The relief that Sheila had assured Duncan would come his way passed him by. His wife's sympathetic, professional stroking of his neck did little to ease the depression which engulfed him. He was too much of a coward ever to re-open his relationship with Margaret and too much of a man ever to forget it. As for Margaret, Duncan was dead and as such she grieved the loss of him, but her subsequent mourning aided her recovery from the loss without giving her lasting or permanent injury. It just suddenly made her feel a lot older than her years. At this stage in her life, she felt about 125 years old.

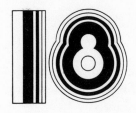

Margaret packed her over-night case in preparation for the journey to Wolhamthorpe Quarter Sessions. Christmas had passed quietly, but not unpleasantly. She glanced at the Callas record that Adrian had given her. Dear Adrian, he was becoming less interesting; all that had changed about him was that he had transferred his adulation from a pop-star to an opera singer and had become thinner than ever because it was chic to do so. Somehow, his generosity still came through and, with luck, he might avoid becoming a snob. He had given Margaret a bottle of expensive scent to pass on to Lena. Written on the tag tied neatly around the package, 'Good Luck – All my love, Adrian.' E.B.-J. had dismissed the gesture as superficial. Margaret felt her attitude to be a little harsh. There was more to Adrian than a whiff of perfume; his flippancy and sartorial elegance he used defensively. She placed the present securely between her tights and knickers within her case and maintained a non-judgmental outlook.

Their friendship had not deepened, but on the other hand, he would jolt her on occasions, interspersing his prattle, by saying something awkward and tender.

'I still like you more than anybody, Margo. I wish I could be in love with you.'

However, it was a sad fact that he did not make her laugh as he used to. Perhaps nowadays he tried too hard. Socially, he seemed dependent on being a court jester. Yet the recollection of past times spent together in Runnock still gave her quiet pleasure.

Sir Vivian had risen at four, although their train was not due to leave Euston until seven. For him, the journey offered no anxieties or fears. His case was full of maps and contingency plans for a full scale evacuation of the population of England to the Isle of Man, if as had been reported, scores of marauders from an alien planet had been infiltrating pasture-land between London and Liverpool. He was well clothed in a heavy military overcoat. An enormous pair of binoculars hung round his neck and for some reason only valid to him, he wore a fez which, by repute, had been given to his father by some grateful or subservient pasha or another.

There was plenty of room in the train. Sir Vivian began to scan the landscape within five minutes of departure, immediately lost in thwarting the only enemies known to him. No such imaginary demons tended Wintner's thoughts. Tight-lipped, white-faced, he shrank into the corner of the compartment and uttered nothing but coughs from a throat which was not sore, but dry with anticipation. Margaret found it difficult to concentrate on the history-book before her. It presented a picture of royalty which continuously soured the previous preconceptions that she had with regard to their inherent goodness. Besides, the click-clacking of E.B.-J.'s knitting needles were at odds with the rhythm of the engine. Eventually, she placed the book aside, closed her eyes and concentrated on knit two purl one. She heard the corridor door bang; this was followed by a faint cough. Wintner had left to collect refreshment from the buffet car. The knitting continued.

'They've got her.'

Startled from her boredom, Margaret jerked her chin from her neck as Sir Vivian spluttered another half shout.

'She's dead, my God, dead.'

E.B.-J. had slumped forward and had almost rolled on to the floor. Sir Vivian held her and Margaret assisted him in laying her comfortably along the carriage seat.

'You're just in time, give me the cup', said Margaret turning to Wintner who hovered in the carriage doorway bewildered and shocked.

'We'd better pull the communication cord, it must be serious. Stella is never unwell. Never.'

Margaret took a plastic beaker from his hand and held it to E.B.-J.'s lips.

'The communication cord, we must pull it', he said.

'Do it then, man, don't dither', said Sir Vivian, who thrived on emergencies.

'It won't be necessary. This is Rugby, the train stops here', said Margaret, the grinding of the brakes serving to verify her words.

E.B.-J. buttoned up her blouse after the young Pakistani doctor had indicated that his examination was complete. Sir Vivian and Wintner conscientiously guarded the door to the ladies' waiting room. The doctor spoke to E.B.-J. who dad been quickly revived with some smelling salts. Her face remained ashen.

'Yes, madam, everything is perfectly all right, absolutely normal, you have nothing to worry about. At this stage, I think it unadvisable to travel a great deal, particularly in the morning.'

Margaret looked at E.B.-J. and then questioned the diagnosis.

'I'm not satisfied, please call for an ambulance, she is never ill. . . .'

'In my country, young lady, pregnancy is not regarded as an illness. Call an ambulance if you wish, but . . .' the doctor seemed a little put out. Margaret, abashed by her own naivety, apologised.

'I'm sorry, I didn't understand. You have been most kind.'

'Thank you and good day.' He nodded a little over-courteously and left.

'I don't want him to know; you won't tell Harry?'

It was the first appeal E.B.-J. had ever made to Margaret.

'Are you happy?'

'Yes, I am. You won't tell?'

'Why not?' Wintner entered. 'Of course I won't', said Margaret.

'Oh, Stella are you all right?'

E.B.J. stood up and smoothed her skirt and straightened her bun.

'Nothing serious', she said and forced a little snigger.

Wintner did not seem assured.

'It was just sickness. Travel sickness', said Margaret. 'A little air will do us all good.'

They all walked to the end of the platform and viewed the railway lines before them. Did the signals change the direction of the trains or did they know where they were going? The lines all seemed to meet anyway. They had plenty of time to think on such matters as the next train to Wolhamthorpe involved a two-hour wait.

E.B.-J. recovered quickly and on arriving at their destination lost no time at all in hailing a taxi and demanding swift conveyance to the courthouse. It was at this point that Margaret began to realise that much more was at stake than Lena's pending captivity or freedom. Friendship was beginning to appear more complex and difficult; it not only involved love, but some curious kind of obligation. Being accountable to one friend might easily mean betraying another. These tangled webs of loyalty worried her. She frowned as she sat in the back seat of the taxi; objectivity did not come easily to a woman of such tender years – she was most uncomfortable with the idea of learning by mistakes. Perplexed by her mood, Sir Vivian took her hand and patted it very gently. His comforting was always registered simply.

It was after midday before the taxi arrived and groups of people dotted the steps of the court.

'Make up yer bloody mind', the taxi driver muttered.

The poor man was somewhat confused.

'Drive back, drive back', bleated Sir Vivian.

'Just pull in over there', said E.B.-J.

Both had seen Lena. 'Do as the lady says', said Wintner.

Lena could not be mistaken, she was the only person standing alone. The strains of the past few months were not reflected in her present style or bearing. Knee length shiny boots and a heavy fur coat protected her from the cold – a felt hat hugged her head and covered her ears, an 's' shaped feather was attached to the right-hand side of the hat, half of the plume sprouted into the hair, the other half swept round her neck. She was having a little trouble fending off pigeons who seemed to mistake the lump of fur and feather for some kind of kindred creature.

Sir Vivian was under no such illusion. He held on to the door of the taxi-cab as the other three tried unsuccessfully to cajole him on to the pavement.

'Driver, take me back to the station. D'you hear man, the station', he roared.

By this time, Lena had observed the consternation and lost no time in joining the group. Harry had begun to tug on Sir Vivian's arm.

'Force won't be necessary, Harry, we can all travel to the station', Lena spoke quietly.

'But. . . .' Lena cut her sister's query short and glided into the corner of the cab.

'Hop in, all of you, I'm free. Quite free.'

They obeyed.

'Driver, the station please', said Lena.

'It's nice to know some bugger knows their own mind around here anyway', the driver spoke with relief.

'Yes, it is, isn't it', said Lena, who had removed her fur mittens and passed her large handbag for Margaret to look after. She did not wait for questions.

'It seems that I have wasted a lot of your time, the case was dismissed within forty minutes of it all starting. A pity really as there was a great deal that I needed to say. I never had a chance to get started, my dears, there is more fussing in a court of law than a hen coop. All the standing up and sitting down, one gets quite dizzy with it.'

She sighed a little too heavily.

'Never mind me, it is so good to see you all together.'

'Dismissed?' E.B.-J.'s question had an empty, enigmatic sound.

Lena ignored it, but answered indirectly.

'What shocks me most, is the wastefulness of it all when you consider the cost of those legal proceedings. I mean the payment of the police, counsel, court officers and all the rest of the inconsequential paraphernalia, then one must either smile as one does at *Alice in Wonderland*, or cry as one does in parts of Dickens' stories.'

Lena blew her nose at this point, but Margaret did not detect any tears behind the ornamental green-framed spectacles.

'I suppose the ending of my little saga is Dickensian in that good has triumphed, yet it saddens me to think that the price of it all must be borne by the state. Three families could have been housed comfortably – permanently – if Percy had decided to dismiss the case before it commenced.'

She paused and, barring the taxi-driver from any more strictures on social conscience by shutting the small window which opened into the driving compartment, she continued.

'It saddened me to see Percy sitting there in that vile hair-do. He was quite handsome once you know.'

'You knew him then?' Of the company present, Margaret alone was surprised that Lena should know a high court judge. The other three were already either crushed by her confidence in herself or overwhelmed by her rhetoric. Sir Vivian had shrunk into a corner of the cab as far away from Lena as possible. Occasionally he would view her like an aged half-dead beast looking at a vulture. Wintner sat opposite her on the fold-up seat. This was causing problems as one of the hinges had broken; from time to time his knees were pushed forward so that they touched Lena's thigh. E.B.-J. looked forlorn as though she were already resigned to some pending mortal loss or dire fate.

'My sister tells me that you are doing well, Margaret.'

Lena had closed her own case, directing her gaze towards Margaret who was now required to fill in time with conversation until the taxi reached the station.

'Yes, I'm getting more than enough work now. At first it was very hard, it's a very competitive business. E.B.-J. has helped me a lot.'

'You will get to the top, my dear, I know it. Fame is written on your liver and you may suffer accordingly. You will achieve what I have tactically avoided, although it is constantly thrown in my path. I will never assent to it because I am not prepared to compete.'

Lena's last sentence almost roused E.B.-J. to challenge, but the taxi rounded the corner of the road at the entrance to the station rather suddenly. E.B.-J. clutched the hand rail and stared hard out of the window.

Sir Vivian once again threatened to immobilise Lena's plans when he refused to accompany her to the Wimpy Bar (there was a forty-minute wait for the London train). The group divided, Wintner now carried Lena's case and E.B.-J. accompanied Sir Vivian across the railway bridge to the platform opposite. Margaret watched the figures reappear and disappear between the framework of iron girders, E.B.-J. placating the old gentleman as he gallantly struggled with her baggage as well as paying mind to his own peculiar accessories. They did not turn to wave. Margaret was surprised at the lack of affection, but when she realised that she was standing alone, she looked round for Lena, who was guiding Wintner by the arm through the glass doors of the café. Evidently, Lena was not going to waste the forty minutes; instinctively, Margaret made her way towards her first tutor.

'How will you manage, Lena? Do you have enough money?'

Wintner's voice trembled with concern as he looked at Lena across the table. Margaret perched herself on a high round stool behind Wintner, it being the nearest seating that she could get. There was no problem in hearing the conversation, but participating would be difficult. Nevertheless, she was able to have a clear aerial view of the proceedings. Lena took Wintner's hands in hers and flashed a smile of assurance.

'I always manage, Harry my darling; as a matter of fact, I have a job to go to at the end of April. No, don't look so pained Harry, it's nothing spectacular, it's so safe, it's dull. I am assisting Carl Daveed in a Summer Season at Morecambe.'

'Assisting in what?' Wintner bit into his hamburger. Lena shook her head.

'Harry, you lack two qualities that are most essential in a man.'

She paused and leaned further forward so that her feather almost encircled his neck. 'Trust and adventure; I shall be Carl's co-director. It seems culture is about to descend on the middle classes, the Corporation plan to present an operetta in one of the many spacious parks in Morecambe. *Hiawatha* seemed an obvious choice. Only part of the cast can be professional. To allow for budgeting we are enrolling forty-three amateurs from local choral societies. If we cover them in war paint and stick them on ponies, they won't cause too much harm as long as they keep singing.' Lena laughed.

Wintner smiled half-heartedly, not yet quite convinced.

'Who is Carl?'

'Darling, I have known him years, his wife is a Catholic and he is Jewish. They have hundreds of children, he always wears the newest arrival slung round his back when he is working. The cast never quarrel with him for fear of waking the baby. When the show ends in mid-September, I leave for the Third World.'

'Where?'

'Africa – North Africa, Morocco to be precise. Before you express your anguish consider me, Harry. I have decided, in spite of my oncoming maturity, to be responsible for teaching English to the children of an eminent Emir.'

This piece of information forced the last piece of hamburger to stick in Wintner's gullet.

'Oh, Lena ...' the onions had also given him wind, he stifled a painful belch.

Lena stroked his jaw.

'I don't have to travel alone. There is a post for an English chauffeur. We could go together, Harry, bound by the jasmine-scented evenings and Mahomet; we could regain what we left in Dalston and more.'

This was too much for Margaret who felt that it was time to speak.

'Were you in business together then?' Lena looked up and gazed over Wintner's head.

'Margaret dear, I hadn't noticed you sitting there.'

Margaret knew this to be untrue. Wintner turned towards Margaret, questioning her with a gaze which said, 'Forgive me, help me.'

Lena asked, 'Well, Harry, are you prepared to accept what you lack – trust and adventure?'

'What did you offer before in Dalston, freedom and passion?

What did they do for him?'

'Margaret, this matter does not concern you.' Lena spoke calmly without anger.

'There's Stella to think of', said Wintner.

'Well think of her then, Harry, think of her. You left her the last time and I helped you to develop into what you are now. I only parted from you afterwards because we had begun to fail to value one another, we had lost our urgency. Can you feel it now, the urgency? You see I am right. Stella can give you nurture it's true. There is no one kinder or more sweet than my sister. But Harry, you know that I offer you life.'

Lena took Harry's hand and held his fingers to her lips, she let go of the fingers when Margaret spoke once more.

'Our train leaves in seven minutes, Wintner, we must cross the bridge on to the other platform or we will miss it.'

Wintner coughed, as was his habit during times of tension.

'Ahem, ahem, I don't think I'll be. . . .' Margaret slithered from the stool.

'If it's life you want, then you've got it, in fact you've made it. There's no need to travel to Morocco.'

'Margaret, I loathe riddles', said Lena.

'I hate empty words', said Margaret.

'You had better get your train, dear. Harry is staying here; perhaps you could let my sister know that I will be contacting her after an "aussi long absence" as the French would say.'

'What life have I made, I'm a follower not a maker, not a doer?' said Wintner, who seemed to be bound for Meknes once more.

'You've done something', said Margaret. 'You've made a baby. Stella's having it – in September.'

Wintner smiled and walked shakily from the café towards the other platform leaving pupil and teacher face to face.

'Why did you do it?' Lena spoke as she tucked her hands into the fur mittens.

'You were competing, it's against your own rules, I'm sorry, Lena.'

Margaret made no move to catch the train. What right had she to interfere? There was no triumph for her in Lena's defeat.

'The baby will make all the difference', said Lena brightly.

'You've lost your dialect.' She paid the bill.

'You must rush, dear, or you will miss your train.'

Margaret called from the entrance.

'I love you, Lena, please believe me.'

'Of course I believe you', she held her hand out to the cashier.

'Don't I?' The cashier gave the change.

'Yes, course she does, duck.'

Lena gave the lady another shilling for her sensitivity as Margaret raced over the bridge.

Lena had begun to wave as the train pulled out but her attention was taken up by a man in a turban who had begun to speak to her.

'Is he Moroccan?' Wintner whispered.

'I think he's a bus-conductor', said Margaret as E.B.-J. began to knit.

'Look', gasped Margaret and pointed to a dishevelled man who was waving a pathetic bunch of broken asters from the end of the platform opposite. Lena turned and began to walk towards him as the train left the platform.

'It's Arthur, he's a pianist.'

By this time, Wintner had lost interest and had begun to attend to Sir Vivian who was foraging around the compartment in search of some lost binoculars.

Margaret gurgled with content. 'He's got the quality.'

'What?' asked E.B.-J., placing her knitting on her lap.

'Arthur the pianist. . . .'

'A pianist!' E.B.-J. shook her head. For someone so young, Margaret did tend to ramble on at times.

'And before I go, I'm going to give you a piece of my mind.'

E.B.-J. heaved herself behind her desk and waited with genuine interest. Mavis had never given her any indication of having a mind before, so it might be as well to know what a piece of it was like before she left.

'I've been with you for five years, treated you like I would my own daughter, and now I'm faced with this kind of insult.'

'You never had a daughter?'

E.B.-J. folded Mavis's insurance cards in an envelope and pushed them towards the end of the desk. She was still waiting for the piece of mind.

'I'm glad I didn't. God knows, if she had turned up with what you've got I would have disowned her. For a woman of your age and status to end up in that condition is not just stupid, it's criminal.'

She took her cards and pocketed them.

'Criminal. I put it all down to that Trixie's influence; things have never been right since she came here.'

Mavis buttoned up her coat and made gestures to leave.

'Here', said E.B.-J. 'There's another £10. Count it as extra holiday money.'

She rested her hands on the distorted stomach and looked at the ungainly paunch which overshadowed part of her desk.

'Margaret had no influence over this, Mavis. It was just me and a man I know that did it.'

Mavis took the money quickly; it did nothing to soften her tone.

'You've no shame neither, I really can't bear to look at you.'

She reached the door and called over her shoulder before opening it.

'Would you like a cup of coffee before I go?'

'No, no, thank you', said E.B.-J. The telephone rang and Mavis left.

E.B.-J. picked up the receiver with one hand and pushed the window behind her open just a little further. The September afternoon was unusually warm and in her present condition the heat discomforted her.

'Awkward Agency, Awkward Agency. Models that are different.' Oh, hell, thought E.B.-J. I've got a breather, as no voice came from the receiver. 'Hello, Awkward Ag . . .'

'Hell-O there, Hello-O there, remember me?' She recognised Larry Bonard.

'Yes, as we do all battle heroes – "lest we forget".'

E.B.-J. decided wisely not to pursue a sarcastic tone. 'I see from various reports, that you are doing very well nowadays. Congratulations.'

'Gee, thanks, but I hear the bouquets are coming your way soon, seems it's never too late to hit the jackpot, eh?' he chuckled into the telephone.

'No never', said E.B.-J. and unbuttoned yet another section of her smock.

'Now, Larry, how can a small family concern like mine help a now thrusting young film director? If you have telephoned to express your goodwill, then I accept it gladly in the spirit it is offered, and I return the compliment; I know in your own way you are as busy as I am and if you will exc. . . .'
He cut in.

'Still the same old Stella. As it happens, you might be able to help me, sugar. In fact, we could help one another.'

E.B.-J. performed her own Yoga and listened more intently.

'I'm – er – I'm – er – looking for a girl, late teens, early twenties, must be quite small, well shaped, but not beautiful. Sex appeal not essential.'

'I wouldn't have thought that was difficult, try Woolworths', E.B.-J. replied drily.

'Wait, wait, baby, gently let me finish. No this girl must have – er – clarity, yeah, clarity, she needs appear to be funny to both men and women and have a kinda' innocent quality – good eyes would help.'

E.B.-J. put her hands to her throat. She did not want to convey to Larry her fears for Margaret. She edged towards flippancy too far.

'By your terms, baby, since when did you meet an innocent model? Larry, I'm afraid I'm wasting your time, I have no one on my books whom I could responsibly recommend.'

'Cut the cackle!'

'Pardon?'

'You heard what I said. I need a chick with integrity, the kind of sweetie who can dissolve a bastard like me with a look. I need her for a film sequence – she's just right for it, I know it. You've got her. If you won't play ball, then I'll arrange the terms for myself. OK?'

E.B.-J. patted her bun.

'You want Margaret – you want Trixie Trash?'

'Yeah.' Larry's Americanisms were interspersed with Chelseaisms now.

'She is in great demand now, her fees are not what. . . .'

'Money's no problem. Allied Enterprises are backing the film, they are anxious for completion – three days' shooting should do it.'

'I'll arrange a contract then tomorrow at two; there is one other thing. Just a small detail. You do realise that her legal guardians must be present throughout filming. The girl is under twenty-one.'

'No, I didn't realise – but it's fine by me. You had better get them organised for next Monday – seven a.m. Battersea Fun Fair. Oh, don't forget to tell them to bring the girl along.'

'Perhaps you had better take their names – the names of the guardians. They are Sir Vivian Bland, OBE, Mr Harry Wintner, and Miss Estelle Bingham-Jones.'

Larry whistled as E.B.-J. announced the trio.

'Wow – she must be some piece of merchandise. Now I understand', said Larry.

'I don't think you do, Mr Bonard, but your understanding is of no importance. Saturday then?'

'It's a deal', said Larry.

E.B.-J. took the stairs carefully and recovered her breath a little at the bottom as she stepped to dump a pile of discarded files amongst the heaps of newspaper awaiting collection in the jaded entrance lobby. She stood with one arm holding on to the banister and would almost certainly have fallen in horror had not the wooden framework lent its support. The newspapers had begun to move. If it were rats, she would keep quite still. There was no need to panic, just keep quite still.

'It takes more than three tiddlers to fill a fish pond, just you try it then, just you try. I'm not without my credentials, don't you come the hoity-toity with me, young man. Hitler is no friend of mine and I am not accepting poison from anybody.'

E.B.-J. looked dispassionately at the ravaged female with glazed eyes and matted hair that had sat up for air. Methylated spirit and stale wine engulfed E.B.-J.'s nostrils. She took two quick steps to the doorway, revolted by what she had seen, she gulped in some fresh air.

'Who did this to you?' E.B.-J. had returned with two ham rolls which she placed near the raddled hump of femininity. She proffered a pound note which was snatched from her.

'Who did it to you – who did it, for Christ's sake?' E.B.-J. shouted.

A policeman peered in the doorway and studied the two women, he addressed E.B.-J.

'She causin' more trouble again, madam? They oughtn't to be allowed around, not good for someone like yourself to have to contend with, I'll move her along.'

'No, leave her, I told her she could stay there for tonight. It's no problem, officer.'

The officer's intentions were kindly and he walked with E.B.-J. to the bottom of the street as she appeared to be a little preoccupied.

'We did it, officer, we did that to her, you and me.' She repeated this phrase before thanking him as he saw her into a home-bound taxi.

Margaret received the news on the forthcoming filming calmly. She went to her room shortly after the evening meal and commenced reading. Her choice of books were indiscriminate, she managed to read at least three a week. This week there was a novel concerning the fortunes of a mill-owning family, a history book on the Russian Revolution and a handbook on Freud. She dipped from one book to another, this habit was the cause of her eventual short-sightedness and astigmatism.

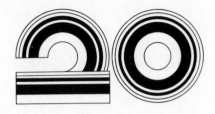

Margaret shook hands with the producer of the film after she had emerged from the make-up department. She was oblivious to the detailed attention given to her by the scores of ancillaries, technicians and extras who thronged the setting. These people were impressed by the trio (who never left her side) as much as by her. The trio scrutinised everything. The old gentleman had even gone so far as to taste her tea before passing it to her. The girl must have some kind of heavy backing, or be potential star material for this kind of intensive chaperoning to be at hand. The pregnant one sat knitting all the way through the director's pre-shooting brief, and listened like a barrister about to defend himself.

Larry Bonard smiled and billed and cooed the way he had when Margaret had met him previously. His jeans had been carefully aged, he had grown a moustache and beard to give him the trace of intellectuality that his new role of director demanded. Everyone around him was treated as an old friend – including Margaret.

'This could be your big chance, sweetie, there are two sequences of seven minutes. One plays behind the credits and the other closes the film. We have Bill Fairfield playing the central character – a writer who is torn to bits by the four women who enter his life. Each successive relationship wounds him more than the one before, but he is involved in the eternal search.'

'It sounds familiar', said Margaret.

Bonard continued.

'Your screen time is short, but vital – he sees you as the unattainable, the enigmatic, the chick that is real, the one that has always eluded him. You get the connection?'

'I am a dream image?'

'No, no', snapped Bonard. 'You must be human, but separate. Tell me, cookie, you tell me yourself. I know you can do it. What makes you feel apart – feel different?'

E.B.-J. stopped knitting and noted Bonard's tenacity. He bent forward and placed his elbows on his knees and whispered his appeal to Margaret.

'If I am searching for myself, I wouldn't notice anyone if they were looking for me, would I? I mean I would be too absorbed to notice.'

Margaret's head tilted slightly to the left as she continued to muse.

'That's it, that's the expression we want, baby', Bonard murmured encouragingly.

'When I was ten, two boys told me where babies came from. You fall from your Mum's fanny they said. It was a terrible shock even when the truth was verified in a gentler fashion later. And when I found out that love-making and sex made babies, I was even more upset. I had worked it all out comfortably that any two friends could have a baby. It was horrible to know that you could have one without even liking the other person. You see, I don't know whether or not my Mum liked my Dad. When I think about this I feel lost and I think about it a lot. I suppose if I find me, then it won't worry me any more. It's easier being other people than being yourself isn't it?'

E.B.-J. spoke gently, not wishing to break Margaret's reverie.

'My dear', she said.

'Perfect, just great. Keep that expression through the shooting. I knew you had what I wanted. What a face! I want some close-ups of the eyes. We'll do the indoor work while it's still light. OK?'

Margaret nodded.

The middle-aged male lead, Bill Fairfield, had almost fallen to the ground in between several attempts to catch a longing look at Margaret before being confounded by mirrors in the crazy house which only reflected a gross distortion of himself when he thought he had finally reached her. Margaret felt that he stumbled too much, that the desperation should have shown in a less physical way. In discussing it later with Wintner and E.B.-J., she had wondered whether or not he had a drink problem.

'He does have a drink problem', said E.B.-J. 'But it's his feet that are giving him hell, not the whisky. Look.'

Margaret and Wintner looked at the star who was being prepared for his next view of his goddess in the Ghost Train.

Two strong rather wilful-looking ladies were pulling him into some cleverly camouflaged corset-trousers that Napoleon might have been proud of which dispersed his stomach paunch. In order that the operation should be effective, he was required to stretch up to his full height and grasp at the iron bar which supported the roof of the marquee. At most, a foot had been added to his height by the strange high blocked shoes. These proved most cruel as they left his calves and ankles in a state of semi-paralysis. His walking resembled the swagger of John Wayne and the gait of Frankenstein's monster. However, it was generally accepted by cinema goers and critics that the man exuded a sombre sex appeal.

During the lunch break, Bill Fairfield congratulated Margaret on her work in the mirror and Ghost Train sequences. He had been extricated from his corset and had donned slippers for his rest break. He spoke beautifully, describing his childhood in the Welsh mining valleys. The people there meant a lot to him. He was deeply sorry that he was forced to live in Geneva, Rome and Beverly Hills most of the time on account of fierce tax demands. He warned Margaret of the dangers of fame and stressed the importance of family life. He called in on his wife at Phwellangollen at least twice a year; her name was Mary, and he called her his insurance policy for old age. Margaret wanted to tell him about Runnock, but it was difficult as the rest of the diners listened to him as if he were the radio. His talking did not cease until the break was over.

'It's been a great pleasure meeting you', he said to Margaret as they left to resume work.

Margaret smiled and nodded. She would have liked to have met him. The small, fat kindly man had reminded her of one of the friendly grocers who worked at the Co-op in Runnock.

'It's a pity he didn't have time to listen', thought Margaret. 'He might have learned to enjoy fishing or growing roses in Geneva, Rome or Beverly Hills.'

'It's called an octopus', said Larry Bonard.

'I don't like the look of the thing, no, not one bit. I don't like it.'

Sir Vivian gave the thick woollen scarf another twist around his neck and peered at E.B.-J. from over his autumn yashmak.

'Neither do I', said E.B.-J.

'I think it's ever so pretty. Oh, they are lighting up the trees.' Margaret pointed to the coloured bulbs which dripped light from the plane trees nearby.

It was dark now and the glare from the cameras enhanced the shadows under E.B.-J.'s eyes and emphasised the redness around her mouth. Wintner had suggested that they might return home, but this plan had been swiftly squashed. There was no question of leaving Margaret alone, however. The group experienced serious misgivings when Margaret was requested to climb into the mechanised octopus unaccompanied.

'This is just a trial run through, sugar. We want you to feel confident and free. This is the joy ride of all time. You get my meaning?'

Margaret nodded and clambered into the semi-circular seating casket which was fixed to the end of one of the dozen iron girders that were to sweep round like tentacles as they clawed the night sky. An old man secured her seat belt and the thing gyrated and spun into action. After Margaret had become accustomed to the fact that she had left her stomach and entrails on the ground, she began to enjoy the journey.

Within half a minute she had spun through expanses of sky, tree-tops, canvas roofs and scanned humans who were intent on watching her hurtle into the darkness. When the machine did stop, she needed some moments to collect her stomach and other parts of her anatomy which felt as though they had been dispersed all over the place. She was pleased with her performance and it surprised her when Larry Bonard greeted her with a deep frown.

'Baby, we have a problem.' He shook his head. 'One helluva problem.'

'What's wrong? I felt free, it didn't worry me.' Margaret touched her face. Had her innate feelings not expressed themselves truly? Larry interpreted the gesture correctly.

'Oh, you were probably fine.' He paused and turned to signal Bill Fairfield into position. 'But we don't know for sure as only the top of your head is in camera. Sorry, baby, I guess you're too small for the part.'

Margaret knew that the bait was set; Larry Bonard had not changed; cruelty was still his business. She answered him quietly, almost casually. She did not wish to convey to him that hir decision had caused her any trace of personal torment.

'I'll stand up if you like, you'll get my arms and torso in view then.'

The old man working the machine shook his head as Bonard accepted the offer.

'Great, what an idea, er – you know it could be kinda er –
dangerous?'

'It had entered my mind but, quite truthfully, I enjoyed the
ride the first time round and one always learns by experience.'

She pointed to the sky.

'I made a few friends up there, I'm sure that they will be
pleased to see me again. Thank you for your concern, Larry. As
always, you are most kind.'

Without waiting for further direction, she climbed into the
casket, planted her feet firmly apart, gripped the iron bar in
front of her and nodded a patronising smile to director and
camera crew to indicate that the star was ready for flight.
E.B.-J. held the swollen sides of her stomach and offered
prayers to any deity available, interspersed with muttered
obscenities and curses on behalf of Larry Bonard.

Shouts of encouragement and applause filtered through to
Margaret from the crowds below helping her to cloak her
fears. She became familiar with the twists and swerves of the
casket as the iron arm which carried it shot up, down and
around the machine's changing perimeter. Her own view of
the space around her had also been improved by embarking
on her second journey through space in this more daring
fashion.

Margaret's new view of the world granted her unusual liberties.
Now free from fear or anxiety, she was only concerned with the
exhilaration which the immediacy of flight was presenting her
with. She released the hand rail and pushed her arms back-
ward, thrusting her neck forward as she did so. I am a swallow,
she thought as she swooped past trees, electric cables and the
striped canvas tops of the marquees and tents. The crowds
below watched in awed silence as the camera continued to
whirr. Knees crouched, hair swept back, her eyes filled with
tears as the fierceness of the wind caught her face; she placed
one arm to her side and extended the other one in a gesture of
salutation or blessing as the casket hurtled relentlessly round. I

am liberty, I am Boadicea, Queen of the Iceni – she thought as once more the iron arm spun upwards.

Now she felt welcoming and opened both arms outwards, embracing the night and the universe. I am Margaret, part of all of this. She smiled, it was better than her first bike ride, better than applause, more exciting than a first kiss, more satisfying even than. . . .

Bonard's voice crackled over the loudspeaker hailer.

'Side cameras in focus, now, shoot, shoot. Don't miss this angle, get the back view, great, just keep going, great.'

The old man working the mechanism shook his head at Bonard and indicated by whispered foul abuse that he would not take responsibility for the situation. A pimply faced youth, who professed that he knew the machine backwards, stood over the controls and pocketed £5.

Two more minutes, which seemed like a life-time to the anxious crowd below, were sufficient in filling Bonard's appetite. Creatively, he was more than satisfied. There was no point in prolonging Margaret's pleasure. If she had been frightened, it might have been a different matter.

'OK, Cut! Cut!' he bawled as Margaret prepared herself for entrance to the firmament.

The pimply faced youth mistook the camera crew's directions for his own and indolently hauled the largest of the three levers towards himself. An agonised scream from the hub of the machine rent the air, the crowd clapped their hands to their ears in unison as the main brake ground on against impossible odds. Cables snapped, light bulbs popped and the arms of the octopus convulsed to a halt with a massive shiver.

'My God! Oh, my God!' Even Bonard's inherent sadism turned to dismay as he watched Margaret soar into orbit as though she had been shot from a cannon. Her line of flight was broken by an aerial somersault before she twisted into a descent which a trampoline instructor would not have complained

175

about. She bounced twice on the canvas roof top before rolling off its edge into the thick black mud six feet below. It was dark, very dark, but no pain, nothing.

'An ambulance, a doctor, the police.' Orders flew and emergency promoted swift action.

E.B.-J., Wintner and Sir Vivian semi-circled the small, still body. Wintner took off his coat and covered it as E.B.-J. knelt beside the head. One of the camera men provided light, casting a brutal beam on the weird Pieta.

'Don't touch her, don't come any nearer', E.B.-J. hissed as Bonard broke through the crowd.

Sir Vivian waved his walking stick. This action gave the other old man present the impetus he needed. His machine lay wrecked and derelict. The rejection of his advice had resulted in catastrophe.

'You bastard, you rotten bastard', he muttered as his gnarled fist crashed into Bonard's face. 'I won the war for you, yer bleeder', he added as his boots crashed into ribs beneath him. Bonard raised himself and began to cough and the aged fairground attendant left him with his injury. The act was viewed without criticism or praise.

'Slowly, don't try to stand up yet, my dear.' Everyone but E.B.-J. gasped with surprise as Margaret made tentative but wobbly efforts to rise.

'Christ, she's lucky to be alive', said Bill Fairfield who was by now truly captivated by Margaret.

'Nonsense', said Sir Vivian curtly. 'A little shocked maybe, perhaps concussed, but no more. Miss Davis is made of sterner stuff than most, it will take more than a flight of fancy to destroy her.'

He stared blankly into the astonished actor's face.

'We are resilient, sir. Resilient.'

Margaret proved his point as she struggled to her feet supported by Wintner and E.B.-J. Spontaneous cheers and applause broke from the crowd as the mud-bespattered face broke into a weak smile.

They were sipping tea from plastic beakers when the ambulance men arrived; Margaret had even managed to sign one or two autographs. Wintner coughed.

'Er, everything seems to be sorted out, er, the person in question, that is the person at risk, is fine now. We don't need you.'

'We do, Harry', E.B.-J. winced and clutched her side.

'What's goin' on? We had an emergency call for an accident.'

'There's no accident. It's a birth, a pending birth', said Margaret coolly.

E.B.-J. winced with pain and pleasure and nodded in agreement.

'I'm sorry, we can only take one passenger, it's regulations you know. Which one of you is the closest? Which one is kith and kin?' The ambulance attendant gently barred the back entrance of the van. E.B.-J. was already settled comfortably within.

'It's my baby', said Wintner who pressed forward and clambered inside.

'Our baby, Harry. Our baby. We all had a share in it.'

E.B.-J. beckoned Sir Vivian and Margaret.

'Our baby, capital', said Sir Vivian.

'How lovely, we are going to have a baby', said Margaret.

Her dirty unorthodox appearance and obvious pleasure melted any trace of officialdom left in the attendant who was already most perplexed by the entourage.

'Well, I suppose you can work it all out when we get to the hospital. Let's hope it's not twins or you'll be deciding who is what by a game of pontoon.'

He smiled and closed the van door.

E.B.-J. groaned occasionally. There was no conversation from the others. Margaret gazed from the darkened windows as the ambulance crossed the Albert Bridge. The sight of the river and the vista it offered left her unmoved. For a strange excitement bound all the travellers closer than ever before. Margaret picked up a lump of hardened mud from the inside of her left nostril and crushed it between her thumb and forefinger until only a trace of dust remained. She brushed it away and felt satisfied. Clearly, birth was more shocking, more thrilling than any adventure that followed on afterwards. It was a big thing to have a share in, Margaret Davis or Trixie Trash, what's it matter who you are as long as. . . .